Amish Under Fire

Ashley Emma

LIKE FREE EBOOKS?

www.AshleyEmmaAuthor.com

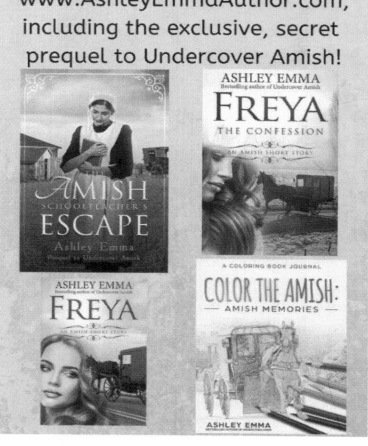

Check out my author Facebook page to see rare photos from when I lived with the Amish in Unity, Maine. Just Search for 'Ashley Emma, author and publisher' on Facebook.

Join my free Facebook group 'The Amish Book Club' where I share free Amish books weekly!

Praise for Amish Under Fire

"Ashley Emma clearly has a passion for the written word. Her knowledge of Amish culture is surpassed only by her love of storytelling. In this follow-up to her bestselling novel, *Undercover Amish*, Ashley weaves a world of passion, danger and intrigue in which a handsome detective must protect a beautiful Amish woman and her young son from her troubled past. I can't wait to read what Ashley writes next."

--Michael Wilkinson, bestselling author of *A Father's Guide to Raising Daughters*

"I LOVE these Amish books by Ashley Emma. They not only grab your interest and keep you reading, they give you a feel like you know a few Amish people and care about them. This is the most powerful step to understanding a culture different from your own. Thanks, Ashley, you have broadened my horizons and you made it fun on the way! There is also a homespun gentleness and honesty about the spiritual side of these differences. If everyone acted like this, Christianity would have a better world view and there would be less hatred in the world. There is nothing more we could ask for from a few books!"

--Chris McKay Pierce, author of *Customer Service Can be Murder*

Excerpt:

"The truth is, we probably won't see you again after your job here is over. That alone will crush my son."

His head dropped. "I'm sorry, Maria." He let out a heavy sigh. "You're right. You're totally right. I know that. But I just can't fight what I feel. I can usually fight off several armed men at once. I fought terrorists in the desert and have fought back shooting assassins in order to protect US senators. But I can't fight my feelings for you, Maria. And I don't want to fight them."

"If things were different..." she murmured, letting him walk closer to her again.

"If things were different, I'd tell you I was falling in love with you," Derek whispered, standing inches away from her.

All was silent except the sound of his breathing. She held her breath, the effect of his closeness freezing every muscle in her body.

"Forget protocol." Derek's eyes dropped to her lips, and his words floated over her softly like a weak summer breeze, shattering all the intentions of walking away that she'd had a moment ago.

She finally breathed in, realization and anticipation pumping through her veins. She shouldn't let him kiss her. This was going too far. What if the stalker came back? What if Derek couldn't do his job because he was distracted and someone got hurt?

But when he leaned in to her, all questions fled her brain and she let herself give in. She ran her hand down his toned arm, over the tattoo of his fallen friends, wanting to know the name of everyone on that list and their stories. She wanted to know everything about Derek. All his untold secrets that lurked in his dark eyes, even the terrible things he had endured on his tours of service.

Everything. All his stories and memories. The imperfect, the gruesome, the beautiful.

TABLE OF CONTENTS

CHAPTER ONE

Maria Mast waited in line at her bank in Portland, Maine, wearing a retro waitress uniform. Her nametag said *Kate,* and she removed it and tucked it away.

Kate was not her real name. Maria had to lie to her boss about a lot of things, but she was grateful for Karen—the benevolent woman who had given her a job and hadn't asked too many questions.

Her boss hadn't pried too much when Maria had shown up for her interview with bruises on her arms. Karen neither pestered Maria about why she didn't talk to anyone about her personal life, nor did she ask why Maria hadn't made friends or trusted anyone. Karen pretended not to take notice when Maria would nervously glance up every time she heard the loud rumbling of a diesel truck pulling into the parking lot.

Even if Karen could have seen the gun concealed under Maria's uniform skirt, Maria wondered if her boss would have even pressed for information about that.

Maria wasn't sure if Karen truly didn't want to pry or was just oblivious, but she was thankful regardless.

The bank teller beckoned to her. Maria slid her cash toward the woman wearing round spectacles. She heard the doors open and

1

screams erupt throughout the busy bank just after depositing the money.

She whirled around. Two armed masked men dressed in all black entered the building.

"Everybody on the floor!" the first criminal shouted while the other stomped over to the tellers, demanding cash.

Maria lowered herself to the floor along with everyone else. Her heart fell into her stomach, anxiety constricting her throat and chest. Maybe nobody would get hurt if everyone did what the men said.

Or maybe she would die here, today, after surviving everything she had already been through. Though she was only twenty-five, she had already withstood more hardship than some people did over an entire lifetime.

What about her son, Carter? Would she ever see him again?

She considered the gun strapped to her leg under her dress. What if she accidentally hit an innocent bystander?

A man had been waiting in line a few people behind her. He was wearing some type of law enforcement uniform—she wasn't sure what kind—with a gun on his hip. The man's hand went to his gun.

"Hey, are you a cop?" one of the robbers asked before the man could even get the gun out of his holster. "You shoot and I'll kill somebody." The bank robber aimed his massive gun at a sobbing bank teller. "Give me the gun, or she dies."

Was that fear that flickered in the robber's eyes? Would he really kill the woman if that man didn't give him the gun?

The man in the uniform reluctantly removed the pistol from its holster. He dropped the magazine and emptied the chamber before slowly handing it to the bank robber. Defeat and indignation darkened his face as he sank to the floor beside the others.

The gunman forced the weeping bank teller to hand over all of the cash available.

"That's all the cash we have," the harried teller with the spectacles cried when the bank robber demanded more cash.

"There's got to be more. Isn't there more?" he shouted.

"No, I swear, that's all of it."

The other gunman grabbed a little girl by the wrist, wrenching her away from her mother as she screamed in terror. He locked her under his arm and held the gun to her head.

"If you don't get us the rest of the cash, I'll blow a hole through her head!" he screamed at the teller, much more confident than the other robber.

Maria's muscles tensed as he shouted. She had to do something.

Her heart pounded harder with each passing second as her fingers reached up to her knee where her M&P Shield was secured in its holster. She slid it out, rested her forefinger along the side of the gun, and clicked off the safety.

The man in the law enforcement uniform caught her eye, looked at the gun, and gave her a nod. His eyes communicated to hers behind black-rimmed rectangle glasses. When she hesitated, he nodded again and jerked his head ever so slightly to the robbers.

Somehow she knew he had a plan. He would help her. All they had to do was create enough of a distraction for it to work.

"Look, the police!" the man shouted, his outburst making the two gunmen turn to the window in a panic.

In the two seconds he gave her, she aimed for the torso and fired, hitting the first gunman by the door in the shoulder.

The man with the glasses lunged toward the other gunman who held the girl, knocking her out of the way. After they moved, Maria hit that gunman in the arm.

Two other men who had been in line leapt into action, swiping the weapons from the two robbers and restraining them as their screams of pain filled the air.

The hours spent at the shooting range had paid off. She had traded some of her paintings for shooting lessons, and her instructor had told her she was a natural.

The man with the glasses looked over at her, admiration in his eyes.

The rest of the people in the bank turned to her, thanking her. Especially the girl's mother, who ran to her crying, throwing her arms around her in a hug.

What if this was reported on the news? What if her face got on TV?

After all her hard work, he would find her. This time, Maria didn't know if he would let her live.

She had to get out of there. She pried the hands of the girl's mother off her and made a beeline for the door, then slammed into someone.

Two strong hands steadied her as she looked up into the face of the man who had helped her.

He let her go and said, "I'm Agent Derek Turner from CPDU. I don't usually wear a uniform, but I was on security duty today for an event. It's a good thing you were here. Are you law enforcement? Why are you carrying a concealed weapon?"

"No, I'm not in law enforcement at all. I took lessons at a range. Look, I have a concealed weapons permit." Maria pulled the permit out of her wallet and handed it to him. "I just want to be able to defend myself."

"I thought maybe you were in law enforcement. That's why I gave the signal to shoot the criminals." He paused. "You saved that girl's life. What's wrong?" he asked. His dark hair was gelled stylishly above a short, stubbly beard, and as he looked into her eyes, she felt as though he could see all of her secrets.

"Everything." She ignored the people thanking her and tried to dart out the door, but two officers blocked her way.

"Wait, miss. We need you to give a statement to CPDU. We need to take you there," one of them said.

Realization that she couldn't get out of this situation washed over her. Panic began to grow within her as she realized this could get her on the news or in public records.

And Trevor might see her on the news and figure out where she was.

Yes, she had saved the little girl's life, but had she just ended her own?

***

"Here's your sandwich, ma'am," Maria said, setting a plate down for a customer in a booth at the Miss Portland Diner. "Is there anything else I can get you?"

"That's all. Thank you," the customer said.

Maria's shift was over. She went out back and hung up her apron, looking forward to going home and taking a hot shower. Today had been one of those days with several difficult customers. To top it off, she'd spilled a drink on one unforgiving patron and she'd mixed up a few orders. Her mind had been clouded since the bank robbery.

She couldn't wait to eat dinner with Carter. Maybe she'd make some popcorn and they would watch a movie afterward.

"Bye, Karen!" Maria called out, grabbing her purse and keys.

"Goodnight, dear," said her boss with a smile.

Nobody from the news had contacted her since the shooting yesterday. Maria had told CPDU that she didn't want to be in the news or in newspapers; she wanted to keep a low profile. They assured her they'd keep her information confidential from the press, like where she lived and worked.

If only Maria had listened to her cousin Olivia Mast when she had first started dating Trevor, maybe she wouldn't be on the run now. Olivia had warned Maria that Trevor seemed controlling, which could lead to abuse.

Olivia, who had left the Amish to become a detective, was like Maria's sister because Maria's parents took her in when her family was killed. The two girls grew up together in the same house like sisters. When Olivia had left the Amish and was shunned, Maria was devastated that she could no longer talk to Olivia. But after Maria left the Amish, they rebuilt their friendship until Trevor made Maria stop talking to Olivia.

Maria opened the diner door and headed outside toward her car.

"We're live. Ms. Mast!" A female news reporter with a cameraman hurried over to her. "Can you tell us what you were thinking when you took down those bank robbers to save that little girl?"

How had they found out where she worked? Had CPDU told them after all?

Maria put her head down and walked faster toward her car, key ready in her hand.

"What you did was so brave, but we want to know more. Where did you learn to shoot? Why were you carrying a concealed weapon?"

"This is America, isn't it?"

Both anger and fear rose within Maria. She unlocked her car and got inside. Did this news reporter have any idea how much she was endangering Maria?

Now it was too late. The damage had been done.

Maria would have to move again.

***

"I need everyone in the situation room, please," Captain Branson of the Covert Police Detectives Unit in Augusta, Maine, bellowed.

Several special agents, bodyguards, detectives, and police officers looked up from what they had been doing.

"Now!"

Everyone started moving more quickly at Branson's sharp tone. Agent Derek Turner had just sat down at his desk to make a few reports from an arrest he had made earlier that day. Now it would have to wait. When Branson said "now," he meant now. All the officers, analysts, bodyguards, and agents milled into the situation room.

Branson cleared his throat as everyone quieted down. "We have received some information on a sex trafficking ring in Portland. We think it might be the same ring that moved from Boston to Portland that we tried to shut down four years ago."

Derek remembered the case well. CPDU had managed to arrest several of the traffickers, but most of them, along with the boss of the trafficking ring, had relocated themselves along with all of the girls they had kidnapped. The trail had gone cold.

He didn't understand how these men could kidnap and profit off of young women. Anger and grief roiled in Derek's stomach, but he clenched his fists and tried to focus on what Branson was saying.

"We think the ring has returned to Portland, possibly after relocating to Boston. We received a tip from someone at the Maine Mall. They suspect that there are young men who are luring in teenage girls by flattering them, spending time with them at the mall, and then offering to drive them home or to a movie. Instead, the men just bring them to the trafficking headquarters. Four girls have gone missing this month at the mall alone." Branson pointed to three photos that had been hung up, all of men in their twenties.

Derek studied the photos, and one of the agents passed copies around the room to everyone.

"We have identified these three men from mall security footage talking to teenage girls multiple times, but we have not located them yet. Garret Fletcher, Ryan Thompson, and Trevor Monroe. We need to be on the lookout for them. If you see any of them, do not arrest them."

"What?" spat one of the newer agents who was known for speaking his mind. "You don't want us to arrest them?"

"No. We need to follow them so that they can hopefully lead us to their temporary headquarters if they are indeed working for the ring." Branson tugged on the belt that was snug under his round belly. "I will assign four agents to go undercover on a mission. We think the traffickers might be keeping the girls temporarily somewhere in Portland. We are trying to pinpoint the location. I am assigning four men to pose as potential 'buyers' while gathering information undercover." Branson made air quotes, making no effort to hide his disgust.

Rage against the traffickers boiled Derek's own blood within him, but he listened intently as Branson continued. He couldn't wait to get to work locating these men and the trafficking headquarters.

Derek tried to listen as Branson continued speaking, but he slowly tuned Branson out. Memories were taking over his mind. The blood on the white carpet of his apartment, the blood on the walls, Natalia's bruised body lying skewed and broken on the floor.

He had been too late to save her. He'd been working when the murder occurred, trying to locate the very traffickers who had been in his own home that night, targeting the love of his life.

The obscene message written on the wall in her blood had been enough evidence to tell them this specific ring had committed the murder out of revenge after Derek had arrested several of their traffickers. Witnesses had also seen the traffickers in the apartment building on the night of the murder.

But they had disappeared, and CPDU hadn't had any significant clues to their whereabouts.

Until now.

"Cristman, Hughes, Rogers, and Smith, I will tell you the details of the mission privately," Branson concluded. "Everyone else is dismissed."

Everyone stood up, and Derek silently chided himself. The meeting was over, and he had zoned out. He hoped he didn't miss any important information. He'd ask one of the others about it later.

Wait. He hadn't been chosen to go on the mission. He was one of the best field agents in the unit. Why hadn't Branson chosen him? Derek's heart hammered. Had he done something wrong? Perplexed, he maneuvered his six-foot frame through the people leaving the room and walked up to the captain.

"You're wondering why I didn't pick you for this assignment," Captain Branson said gruffly, turning to Derek and looking up at him.

"Yes, sir. I'm just wondering why."

"These are most likely the same men who killed your wife. They know what you look like, so you can't work on this case and go undercover. The other thing is the mission will take place on the fourth anniversary of your wife's death. I didn't want you to be distracted,

11

that's all. You are human, just like the rest of us. Distractions can lead to fatal mistakes," Branson said. "Remember two years ago?"

Derek nodded solemnly. He had been so distracted by grief that he had almost let a suspect escape custody. "That was then. I won't make the same mistake again."

"I know you want the same thing as everyone else, which is to catch these guys. So I need you to do something else."

"Yes, sir." Derek slumped and looked at the floor, but he accepted his captain's decision. If Branson thought this was best, then Derek would comply.

"A woman just walked in here, Maria Mast, the woman who shot those two bank robbers. She claims her ex-boyfriend is abusing her. He is one of the traffickers we saw on the mall security footage who is kidnapping teenage girls, Trevor Monroe. Maria is Detective Olivia Troyer's cousin."

Olivia and her husband Isaac had been temporarily transferred to work on a case.

"Go talk to her and get as much information from her as you can. Let's arrest this trafficker," Branson said, tugging on his belt once more, his bald head gleaming in the light from the ceiling. "See if she can help us find out where their headquarters is. She might know where Monroe is. Report to me afterward. Go."

Branson turned to the four agents he had picked and began discussing the details of the mission.

12

Derek respected his boss and his boss' decision, but when he saw that his friend Agent Chris Hughes was one of the chosen, Derek could not deny that he felt a twinge of jealousy. They had worked together for a few years now. Hughes was good in the field, but Derek knew he was even better. Even though he was only twenty-nine, Derek already had more experience than many of the other agents, thanks to his service in the military.

This didn't seem fair. Now Derek was stuck gathering information and pushing papers while his coworkers got to do the really important work. At least he would get to see how the brave woman from the bank robbery was doing. He was glad to help her with her problem ex. This work was important too.

He walked to the front of the building to take the woman into his office. He stepped into the waiting room and said, "Maria Mast?"

A young boy held a coloring book and the woman's hand, his brown eyes glancing around behind his round glasses, taking in CPDU with fascination. Derek smiled, and then he looked at the boy's mother.

The young woman walked toward him. Her long hair was highlighted a lovely shade of honey blonde, falling in loose curls that framed her beautiful face. She wore a simple gray sweater dress that might as well have been a ball gown; it looked so wonderful on her. As she walked, her black heels clacked on the marble floor. She appeared to be a few years younger than him, maybe in her mid-

13

twenties. However, her brown eyes held fear, hurt, and secrets beyond her years that intrigued Derek. And where had she learned to shoot and handle a weapon so well?

Speak, you fool, he told himself when she looked at him expectantly. His mind drew a blank.

"You told them where I worked, didn't you? You saw that I worked at Miss Portland Diner from my uniform?" Fear shadowed her already dark eyes.

"Who?"

"The news reporters."

"No, of course not. Several news stations contacted me about the robbery, asking me for information about the woman who saved that girl the other day," he said after finally regaining his composure. "But I didn't give them any information about you, as you asked. There were plenty of people in that bank. Someone else must have told them."

"Well, whoever told them, the reporters found me at work and put me on TV even though I ran away, covering my face. That's why I'm here. I need help."

This woman intrigued him more and more. "Follow me, please." He led her to his cubicle, awkwardly clearing his throat, which suddenly felt like it had a cotton ball in it.

"Is there someone who could watch my son while we speak?" Maria asked. Quietly, she added, "I don't want him to hear what we will be discussing."

"Oh, I understand. You can leave him with Betty," Derek said, turning to the woman at the desk. "Would you mind watching him while I speak to Ms. Mast?"

"Not a problem," said the receptionist.

"His name is Carter," Maria said and then turned to her son. "Stay with this nice lady for a few minutes until I'm done, okay? Listen to whatever she tells you."

"Okay, Mom," the boy said quietly and went to the front desk. He sat in a chair that the receptionist pulled out for him and opened a farm coloring book.

Maria followed Derek to his desk and sat down in the chair he offered her. She looked at him as he settled into his chair. His dark eyes searched hers, his thick dark eyebrows drawn in concentration.

"So. My boss tells me you are having problems with your ex-boyfriend."

"Yes. Trevor Monroe. He's abusive. I've been on the run from him for two years, but he did this when he found me last night." She pulled back her thick hair to show Derek bruises on her neck, and he clenched his fists as indignation filled him. "He has been to jail for domestic violence before, but someone brought him the money to bail

15

himself out. I don't know who did it. None of his friends seem to have that kind of money.

"Most of his anger was directed toward me when we were together. Though I never lived with him, I broke up with him two years ago and left him to protect myself and my son most of all. Trevor isn't Carter's father, by the way. I moved and have been working under a fake identity. He went to the diner where I work after he saw me on the news the other day, asking my coworkers where I lived, even though I asked them not to tell anyone anything about me. He could charm the socks off anyone and get them to tell him what he wants to know. Well, last night he found me and attacked me. I have a protection order against him, but he is always gone before the police arrive. They haven't been able to catch him. He's too quick, too smart."

"Many women don't report their partner's abuse because they are too afraid or they think it is their own fault."

"I was always afraid to go on the run because he told me if I ever left him that he'd find me and kill me. But last night he didn't kill me. I think he was just trying to scare me again. But next time he might actually do it."

"Sometimes men like him use that as a control tactic. He was trying to prevent you from leaving him. You were brave to report him and leave him. That was a huge risk. However, we may not have found a connection between him and the sex trafficking ring in Portland if he had not been arrested again before today," Derek's deep voice rumbled as he leaned forward on his desk.

He crossed his tan, muscular arms in front of him. Maria looked away as a lovely blush rose to her cheeks. "Do you know if your ex has been involved in human trafficking?" he asked.

"What are you talking about?" she asked, making a production out of smoothing imaginary wrinkles on her skirt.

Derek raised an eyebrow. Was she hiding something?

"Human trafficking—modern day slavery. Not enough people are aware that slavery is still rampant, constantly spreading. Not just in other countries, but here in the United States, especially sex trafficking of women and children. We think Monroe is working for a sex trafficking ring in Portland by luring in teen girls. Do you have any reason to think that he would be involved in human trafficking or any other similar illegal activity?"

"No. I don't think so. Trevor may be violent, but he would never do anything like that," she said. "I don't think he'd hurt young girls."

Sadly, her reaction was typical. Battered women often defended their abusers. Sometimes women even wanted to go back after leaving them, believing that they needed their destructive partner to love them, falling prey to the abuser's brainwashing. He was thankful that she hadn't waited too long to make a report.

At least this woman had escaped to protect her son. She was one of the few.

17

"Well, we think we might have Trevor on Maine Mall surveillance footage luring teenage girls to get into cars with him so he can drive them to a sex trafficking hideout," Derek told her. "He may be guilty of kidnapping, among other crimes. He'd go to jail for a long time if we can prove it. Much longer than if he was only charged with domestic abuse. This time, he would stay in jail for good."

Her eyes widened. "You really think it's him?" Then she said more to herself, "He would do something like that? I mean, I know he is cruel, but this is so despicable."

"Here. I'll show you a short clip of the footage. Let's see if you can identify him," Derek said. He pulled up the surveillance footage on his computer and turned the screen toward Maria.

He played a few seconds of the video and Maria watched as the man on the screen flirted with a young girl who couldn't be older than fourteen. Derek zoomed in on the man's face.

"That's him. That's Trevor Monroe. I'm a hundred percent sure," Maria said.

"Thank you, ma'am. Do you have any more evidence of his abuse? Recordings, videos, maybe?"

"Only bruises," she said, tucking a brown and blonde wisp of hair behind her ear.

"We should also have more solid evidence. Like a recording. We can come to your house to install surveillance," Derek said, even though he knew in his gut that Trevor was guilty of abuse as well as kidnapping. "I could arrest him for domestic violence and endangering the welfare of a child now. However, he might go to jail for a much shorter amount of time. I have an idea. I completely understand if you don't want to do it."

"What do you want me to do?"

"It might be better for you if we wait and also arrest him for kidnapping. If we can prove that he was involved in the trafficking, he'd go to jail for a very, very long time and you'd be safe. You might be able to help us follow him to the trafficking hideout. Where do you live?"

"Just a few minutes from here."

"Here's my idea. What do you think about using him to help us find the kidnapped girls?" Guilt rose within him for even asking her.

"What do you mean? Would I have to see him again? I really don't want to see him ever again. Honestly, I'm afraid for my life."

"I understand, Ms. Mast. However, we would be right outside if anything happened and we'd be listening. We'd be in the house within seconds. You could help us find all those girls that he helped kidnap. It could put him in prison for a long time, and then you and Carter would be safe. Now, I can tell you the plan, but I understand if you need some time to think about it."

Her eyes lit up with hope. "Tell me what I'd have to do first."

For the first time since he met her, all the shadows of worry that shrouded her face were lifted. And she was delightful.

"We've been trying to find out where he lives, and we can't figure it out. Do you know where he lives?" he asked.

"No. I think he moved recently."

"Okay. That explains it. Do you have his phone number?"

Maria pulled out her cellphone. "Yes. He called me after he attacked me, threatening me." She slid the phone across the desk and pointed to one of the numbers on the screen. "That's the number he used."

Derek wrote it down. "Thank you, Ms. Mast. Now, here's what we would need you to do. We're going to set a trap. For the next week or two, we will have an unmarked patrol car parked and hidden by your house, waiting for the next time he goes there. Then we will follow him. Hopefully, he will eventually lead us to where the girls are located. Then, we might be able to use him to shut down this entire trafficking ring. Write down your address here," he said, handing her a pen and paper. "I know this would be hard, but you could help save several girls from slavery."

She nodded slowly, writing. "I understand, Agent Turner. Actually, I can get him to come to my house. When he attacked me, he made it pretty clear that he wanted me back. He thinks he owns me. I could invite him over for dinner to 'talk about our relationship'," she said to Derek, then took her phone back when he was done writing down the number.

Now that she was closer, he could see flecks of gold in her soft brown eyes. He knew there must be so many untold stories and secrets hidden within her. He had to admit that he was curious. He wondered how many times she had tried to leave her ex-boyfriend, and about the many times he had threatened to kill her that made her so afraid of him.

Even so, she was brave. Brave enough to tell someone about it. Many battered women did not get that far.

He wanted to help her so much more than this. Wanted to follow her home and make sure she would be safe by arresting her jerk of an ex-boyfriend, then teaching him a lesson about what happens to men who hit women.

Derek continued, "Yes, Ms. Mast, that would work. As I said, if he goes to jail now, we might not be able to find the hideout otherwise, at least for a while. So, if he hurts you, we will be able to prove he is abusive and he will go to jail for domestic violence. But if we can follow him home, he might eventually lead us to the ring or at least give us a clue to where it could be. You would be safe for good once we arrest him for kidnapping. Here's my card for CPDU." He handed her a business card. "And of course we can arrange for a CPDU agent or officer to take care of your son during the mission."

"He is always with me. Trevor will know something is up if Carter is gone. He knows I don't trust any babysitters. I've always been afraid Trevor would try to take Carter from the babysitter or try to get information from them."

Derek crossed his arms. "I won't allow a child to be endangered in this situation. You'll have to tell him Carter is at a friend's house. You have to make something up."

"What if he doesn't believe me? What if I blow it?"

"Listen, we are asking a lot of you. I know this is hard. Just tell Trevor that Carter made a good friend at school and you got to know them really well and you trust them enough to let him go to their house. That is believable."

"Okay. I'm a bad liar, though. But I will try. I do want Carter to be safe and out of the house while this happens."

"He will be safe with one of our own. I promise."

Maria sighed. "All right. Thank you."

"Of course, Ms. Mast. I will ask to be the one in the patrol car near your house tonight. I can send someone to put surveillance in your house right now if you are going home. This is my cell phone number. Call me anytime, night or day. I'd be glad to help with whatever you need."

He didn't sleep much anymore since Natalia died anyway. He wouldn't have minded if Maria called him at 2:00 in the morning.

"Listen. We'll all understand if you don't want to do this," he told her gently. "It's very brave of you to even consider it."

22

Maria observed his business card. She looked up at him, a little more confident now. "Thank you, Agent Turner. I'll take tonight to think about it and let you know tomorrow if that's okay."

"Absolutely. Now, I have a few more questions I need to ask you," Derek said, and he questioned her for several more minutes. Maria didn't know the answers to most of his questions.

When they finished up, Derek said, "Thank you very much for your cooperation. I'll be waiting for your call, Ms. Mast."

"And thank you. We'll talk soon." She stood up and he walked her out, watching as Carter's face lit up when he saw his mother. The small boy ran to Maria and hugged her waist.

"Thank you again," she said to both Derek and the receptionist.

Derek sent a surveillance technician with her and found himself watching her leave through the large glass doors before going to Branson's office. He knocked on the office door then went inside.

"Well?" Branson asked around a mouthful of potato chips.

"Well, her ex-boyfriend definitely attacked her and is abusive, all right. But I know that the more concrete evidence we have, the better. She agreed to think about it tonight and let us know tomorrow. If she agrees, she would let us know when he leaves the house so we can try to follow him to the trafficking headquarters."

"That's a great idea. He could lead us right to where they are keeping the victims, maybe even the boss. Did you tell her if she feels uncomfortable that she doesn't have to do it?"

"Yes. She knows she doesn't have to, but I think she will. She wants to help shut down the ring, and she wants her ex to go to prison for a long time. I told her we would keep a patrol car outside her house."

"Hate to use her like this, but she could save several girls if she helps us find the right place," Branson said, dropping several crumbs onto his rotund belly. "And I would like to see that scumbag ex of hers go to prison, too."

"With your permission I would like to be the one in the patrol car outside her house, starting tonight." He remembered the tortured look in her eyes, and wondered if she'd be okay tonight. If anything happened, he would be right there for her.

Don't let it get personal, he told himself.

"Yes, of course. Good work, Turner. Thank you," Branson said, waving him away, then reached deep into the chip bag like a bear rummaging through a barrel of fish.

Derek turned to go back to his desk and write his reports, trying to get the beautiful, mysterious blonde woman out of his head.

***

Trevor? Involved in human trafficking? Maria's mind spun with questions as she walked toward her car with Carter. She had no idea Trevor was that malicious, but the more she thought about it, the more she believed it.

A few minutes later Maria pulled into the driveway of their tiny house. It was so small that one might think it was a shed at first glance. The outside wasn't completely painted, and because Maria didn't have time and figured she might have to move again, she never bothered finishing it.

She helped Carter out of his seat and they went inside. Maria started to make dinner, and Carter sat on the floor, coloring in his farm animals coloring book.

As she chopped vegetables, her mind was overtaken with thoughts of how she would make her decision. Should she risk her life to help the kidnapped girls? The thought of seeing Trevor again and having him in her house made her stomach clench in fear.

He had threatened to kill her. What if he really did kill her this time?

Yes, CPDU would be right outside. But would they be able to stop him in time? He was quick and smart. And what if he figured out that CPDU was there and it was a setup?

He would surely kill her. The very thought of imagining Carter motherless sent waves of sorrow through her.

Maybe she couldn't do this. Maybe it was too much of a risk. Maria had spent so long running from Trevor, and Agent Turner was asking her to face her biggest fear head on. Maybe it was too much to ask of her.

As Maria poured the chopped vegetables into a pan, guilt rained on her. How could she be feeling so afraid when the women CPDU was asking her to help find were probably so much more afraid? And facing circumstances that were much more terrible?

Though Maria had been through some hard times, she couldn't even imagine what they were going through.

These girls and women were just like her. She could have been one of them. Trevor could have lured her into the sex trade. In fact, why hadn't he? She had been so vulnerable and naïve; she had trusted him. He could have easily taken her.

Maybe he wasn't involved in that activity at the time. Or maybe he'd wanted her to himself.

Maria had the fleeting thought that maybe he had been trying to protect her, but there was no chance of that. Trevor thought of no one but himself.

"What's wrong, Mom?" Carter asked from where he sat on the floor, several crayons clutched in his pudgy, adorable fingers.

"Nothing, baby. I'm just thinking about a lot of things."

Carter continued his coloring as the war waged on in Maria's mind. Should she help CPDU or not? Should she risk her life for this?

Then it hit her. If she didn't do this, she would spend the rest of her life wondering what would have happened if she had helped them. She'd feel guilty, knowing she could have put aside her fear and selfishness and at least tried to help.

She had to do this. It would be risky, but at least Carter wouldn't be in the house. She would be the only one in danger.

Yes, she was terrified to face her enemy. Yes, he might try to kill her or even succeed.

Maria pulled her phone out of her pocket and selected Agent Turner's number that she had saved in her phone. The phone rang.

"Agent Turner," he answered promptly.

"Hi. This is Maria Mast. I was in to see you today."

"Yes, of course, Ms. Mast. How can I help you?"

"I'm just calling to tell you I made my decision," she said.

"Already? What have you decided?"

"I want to help you. I want to help you find the trafficking headquarters."

CHAPTER TWO

"What is this man doing here, Mom?" Carter asked Maria the next day. He stood at the window of their house, playing with his toy horse as he watched the surveillance technician get out of his car.

"He's just here to fix something. Go play upstairs for a bit until I call you down, ok?"

She had to have him go upstairs to be safe. The less Carter witnessed, the better. He was so observant; she knew she wouldn't be able to prevent him from seeing what was going on unless he was upstairs.

"You can play a game on my phone while he's here," she added, handing him her phone, hoping it would be enough of a distraction.

"Okay," he said as he turned on the game and walked upstairs.

Maria rushed to the door and let the technician inside. He showed her the tiny cameras that were invisible to the unknowing eye and how she could turn them off once Trevor left.

"If the suspect is not arrested tonight and ends up leaving, we won't need the surveillance anymore, so you can turn it off. We only need to see what's going on when the suspect is here. We don't want to infringe on your privacy," the technician told her.

"They are so tiny!" she marveled, staring at the hidden cameras.

"Oh, yes. The suspect will have no idea he is being recorded."

She thanked him. He finished up a while later, then packed up his things and left.

Another car pulled up in her driveway and she tensed, wondering who it could be. She let out a breath of relief when Agent Turner stepped out of the unmarked vehicle. He knocked on her door, and she let him in.

"How are you, Ms. Mast?" he asked.

"I'm good. A little nervous though."

"I assure you, Ms. Mast, you will be safe with us here. I'll park my car in the trees over there on that side of the house. I, along with the other officers accompanying me, will be able to see and hear everything going on inside. We'll be inside in only a few seconds if you think that he starts to suspect anything, or you get uncomfortable at all. I wish I could park closer, but the only area that will cover my car well is over there," Derek explained, referring to a thick patch of trees and bushes at the edge of the woods that could be seen through the window. "Also, I wish we could have agents or officers in the house, but the house is small. We don't want to blow the mission and risk Trevor finding one of us. But we will be close by."

"It's okay, I understand."

"So if you do want us in there, just say the words, 'I made dessert.' Okay? We will be inside within a matter of seconds." He looked into her eyes with assurance, easing some of her tension.

She nodded, and his words made her feel safe. *He* made her feel safe. "Thanks for doing this, Agent Turner."

"No. Thank you, Ms. Mast. CPDU understands what a risk this is for you. If this works, you will be a huge help in finding those missing girls."

Another vehicle arrived, and Derek let a male officer and a female agent in the house.

Derek said, "Carter needs to go with our people now. We assigned two of our most experienced to take care of him. This is Agent West and Officer Sprat. They will be in this unmarked police car, and they are going to take Carter to CPDU headquarters until this is over. Ms. Mast, Carter will be in very good hands. I trust these two with my life."

That was good to hear. She didn't trust just anyone with her son.

The agent and officer shook Maria's hand, greeting her.

"Thank you. I'll go get Carter. He'll love to see the inside of the car." Maria called Carter downstairs. "Carter, these nice people outside are going to show you their police car. Would you like to see it?"

"Yes!" Carter cried as everyone went outside. Maria kissed Carter's forehead and hugged him. "They are going to take care of you for a little bit and then I'll see you later, okay?"

Maria knew she'd see him soon, but her eyes still stung with tears. Who knew what would happen over the next few hours? She hugged her precious son again, stroking his soft hair.

"I love you, Mommy."

"I love you too, baby."

Agent West and Officer Sprat led the grinning boy to the police car. When they opened the door, Carter giggled with delight. "Look at all the buttons!"

Maria smiled a little, relieved that Carter was in good hands and would be having fun. The agent and officer moved his booster seat from Maria's car to theirs, helped the boy inside, then drove away.

Derek let out a long breath. "The other officers and I will go wait in my car. Turn on the equipment when he pulls up."

"Okay."

Derek parked his car in the bushes, and Maria walked inside the house, sighing as she looked around. She kept the place spotless, even though it was very small and cramped. It was all she could afford.

Carter often pulled out his plastic farm animals onto the living room floor. He was obsessed with farms. That was comforting and sentimental to Maria. She missed the simplicity of her former life.

Maria had introduced him to the wonders of the farm world, and ever since then he had been fascinated.

He was such a sweet boy, always cheerful. Carter was smart, too. He could read well, even write well for his age, and he knew a lot about farm animals. He could solve problems and puzzles quickly. Maria knew that he was special and extremely intelligent.

Carter needed a more stable, loving environment, and Maria was determined to give it to him.

Her heart exploded with love for him, and she would do anything for him. She imagined the way his intent brown eyes squinted with concentration as he played. Then, she imagined a smile coming over his slightly pudgy, kissable cheeks. He was probably having a blast looking at the inside of the police car.

As Maria began preparing dinner, she knew the technician had assured her that Trevor wouldn't see the devices. Yet, she was still fearful. He was smart. There was a chance he would suspect that he was somehow being watched.

She prayed to God that Trevor wouldn't find the cameras.

When Maria met Trevor Monroe at a local grocery store and started dating him, she had thought Trevor was everything a girl could want. He was handsome, charming, sweet, and she never guessed he would do anything to hurt her or her baby.

He had told her all the right things at the right time, flattered her, and even told her that he loved her. Trevor had taken advantage of her grief, telling her exactly what she had wanted to hear.

She had believed him. It had been the worst mistake of her life.

Now she wished more than ever that she had never dated Trevor at all but instead had raised Carter in her hometown of Unity, Maine.

She had wanted to return home, but she became too afraid, especially when Trevor repeatedly threatened to kill her and take Carter if she ever left him. Besides, even if she did make it to Unity, she was worried that he would track her down, even though she had never told him or anyone else here where she was from.

No. She had to do this the right way to get her proof. She couldn't just do this halfway.

After she put homemade garlic bread in the oven, she leaned against the counter, worry churning her stomach. If Trevor found the listening device…

Maria looked up above the cabinet where she had hidden one device. She turned it on. He'd arrive any minute.

Please, God, don't let him find it. Please.

She set the table and made a salad. Even though she was indoors, she wore black heels. He always expected her to look dressed up at all times, and if she wasn't, he told her she was too lazy to look presentable. Or he would tell her that she just looked ugly. So she kept her shoes on.

It wasn't worth the criticism. Not today.

Trevor's vehicle rumbled up the driveway. His door slammed; the sound of footsteps followed. He knocked on the door. Every muscle in Maria's body tensed as she opened it. She reminded herself of Derek, who was waiting right outside the house, listening for any indication that she needed his help.

"Oh, good. You're just in time. How are you?" she asked sweetly, trying to slow her heart rate as she opened the door.

Trevor grumbled, kicking off his boots. "Exhausted," he said, plopping down at the table. He looked around. "This is a nice little place you have here. You should have invited me over sooner."

"Thank you. Yes, I should have." Maria pulled the chicken parmesan out of the oven and made Trevor a plate, complete with garlic bread. She made him a salad with ranch dressing and no tomatoes, just the way he liked it.

Those poor girls... This is for the missing girls, she told herself and relaxed a little.

"Where's Carter?" Trevor said.

"He's at a friend's house."

"Really? You never trust anyone with him."

"Well, they've been friends for a while now, so I trust this family. He's only there for a few hours."

Trevor paused, looking at her through squinted eyes. Could he tell she was lying? "What did you do today?"

Maria made herself a plate, her back to Trevor. "I went to the grocery store, went to work, and cleaned the house," she said. It was true.

"Anything else?"

"No. Not really," she said, sitting down. "Paid some bills, too." Her voice shook a little and she stared at her plate.

She just couldn't look at him. He would see the fear in her eyes. She was a horrible liar.

When they had been together, Trevor used to ask Carter what Maria had done that day to try to catch her in a lie. Maria had hated how Trevor put Carter in the middle like that.

Before, Trevor had consistently checked Maria's email, texts and phone calls to make sure that she didn't talk to her family, or anyone else for that matter. Not that her family was allowed to speak to her anyway, thanks to the shunning.

There was no one to talk to because she was too afraid to get anyone else involved in her life. Her family had shunned her, and she had no true friends. She was too afraid to get too close to anyone, worried that Trevor would get to them.

"What happened today? Is Carter really at his friend's house? I know there's something you're not telling me." She turned to Trevor as he crossed his arms, scowling. "He's always with you."

Even her own words sounded pathetic to her. "It's nothing, Trevor. Nothing happened."

"You know I hate it when you lie to me."

"Yes, I know. I'm not."

"What aren't you telling me? Maria, why are you lying to me?" Trevor stood up and roared, leaning over the table.

Maria knew that look.

Panic filled her at the sight of Trevor's anger-filled eyes boring into her, and she uttered the words, "I made dessert," right before Trevor lunged at her.

Pain exploded on the side of Maria's face as she hit the floor. The room spun and blurred before her as it took her a second to figure out which way was up.

A small side table clattered over, creating a huge crashing noise as Trevor attacked Maria again. She tried to scramble away, but he was stronger than her, and the room was still spinning. If she could just reach the kitchen cabinet... The more she reached for it, the farther away it seemed.

Her hand almost brushed the cabinet handle when Trevor grabbed her arms and pulled her toward him. He pinned her down and wrapped his hands around her neck. She felt on the floor for something with which she could defend herself, and she felt sharp broken glass from a shattered vase under her fingers. She grabbed a large piece of glass and cut Trevor's arm.

He cried out, let go of her neck, and grabbed his arm, trying to slow the bleeding.

She crawled toward the kitchen cabinets, hoping to grab a cast iron frying pan.

CPDU agents and officers stormed through the door, guns drawn. "Freeze! Police!"

They surrounded Trevor, and Derek handcuffed him while another officer held him down.

It had been recorded. All of it. Trevor's threats, his abuse, everything. Now she had her proof, and she felt victorious.

CHAPTER THREE

"I made dessert."

Derek was already hurtling into motion, running toward the house. Sitting there listening to how Trevor treated Maria had been torture. He couldn't stop himself from running to her before she said the code words. She had waited too long to say them.

They didn't have the option of following Trevor to the trafficking headquarters anymore, but Derek didn't want to leave Maria with that jerk for another minute longer.

In his line of work, Derek had seen many disturbing things, abuse being one of them. Every time it made him wonder how a person could hurt a child or hit another person. By now, he should have been unaffected. Every time, it still angered him.

Only a few seconds after leaving his car, he and his coworkers entered the house and handcuffed the abuser.

A side table had been knocked over and there was broken glass on the floor. The dining table was set with untouched plates of salad, garlic bread and chicken parmesan. He was starving, and it smelled wonderful. Ever since Natalia had died he had been eating take out or microwave meals. His cooking skills were about as good as a toddler's.

It looked as though they hadn't even begun eating before Trevor lost his temper. Derek and another officer searched him, then the other officers brought him outside to wait for the ambulance.

***

"Are you hurt?" Derek asked.

"I'll be okay," Maria said.

"You have a cut on your cheek. The ambulance will be here soon, and they can take a look at you." Derek touched her face, wiping away the blood.

It was such a sudden, tender gesture. She froze in shock, unable to breathe or move or speak. Her heart rate doubled, yet at the same time, a sense of peace settled over her.

Then in the next moment it was over, like it had never happened. Derek stood up to his full height.

That was weird, Maria thought, baffled by the agent's odd behavior.

He towered over her, but she didn't feel intimidated.

"Thank you for your help, Maria. I'll get the first aid kit for you." Awkwardly, Derek cleared his throat, and he shuffled quickly away.

***

Derek mentally kicked himself. How could he have done that? He felt his face warm at the memory of touching Maria's face.

Anyone could see that Maria was beautiful and kind. Derek's heart clenched when he thought of how she had escaped the abuse of such a violent man.

That had to be the extent of it. He felt bad for her and wanted to help.

He had already slipped after knowing her less than a day. How had he let himself caress her cheek and get so carried away? He had been caught up in the moment.

All agents and detectives in CPDU knew to never let a case get personal. But sometimes it happened, and jobs were lost because of it. Sometimes even lives were lost.

He had worked too hard to be where he was today in his career. He wouldn't let anything jeopardize it.

Derek looked around the house. It was smaller than he had first realized. Much smaller than the average house. It was two stories, but tiny. The home was very tidy and organized, despite its shabbiness. It was decorated with thrift store curtains, vases and rugs. Maria had clearly tried to make the best of things.

Maria approached him. "I'm so sorry I blew it. I wanted to help you find the hideout, but I was afraid Trevor was going to kill me this time."

"No. Don't be sorry. I shouldn't have asked you to help. I apologize."

"I wanted to help! You couldn't have talked me out of it. When I thought of how afraid those girls and women must be, I knew I could see him one last time if it meant that those girls could be rescued."

Derek stared at her, strength and determination burning in her eyes. For a moment, her thick blonde hair reminded him of an untamed lioness's mane, a blazing statement of her steadfastness. She harbored unspoken terrors that he would probably never learn about.

Derek let out a long breath. Even though he dealt with criminals on a daily basis, he would never fully understand people like Trevor.

He was certain of one thing: Maria and Carter didn't deserve this.

"It's all over for you now," Derek said. "Well, part of it, at least. Of course, you will have to testify in court later on, but you are safe now that Trevor has been arrested. What will you do now?"

"I'm going to move back home with my family. I haven't seen them since before Carter was a toddler. Over three years."

"Why? Do they live far away then?"

"No…" Maria sighed. "They live in Unity. It's about an hour and a half away."

"So why not just go visit them?"

"I grew up Amish, and when I left, they all shunned me, which means they can't talk to me," she explained. "But I'm planning to go back and rejoin the church. Once someone repents, they are immediately welcomed back. It would be a good place to raise Carter. I loved living there, and I love my family. It's the best thing for us."

"That's good, then. I'm glad you've decided what to do."

"I'm just sorry I couldn't help CPDU use Trevor to find the trafficking headquarters." Maria hung her head.

"No, no. You did as much as you could. There was no way we could have asked you to put yourself in danger by living with that man for another minute. We'll find the hideout another way," Derek assured her. "We have other men on the security footage that we will attempt to follow."

"That's good to hear. I really hope you find it. I still have a hard time believing my ex-boyfriend was involved in such a heinous crime." She shivered.

Red lights flashed as the ambulance drove up the driveway. "You should get checked out before they take him away. CPDU will transport Trevor to the hospital with an officer in the ambulance. He'll be gone soon."

"Thanks for all you've done, Agent Turner."

"Just doing my job, Ms. Mast. Really, please let me know if I can help you with anything else. You've got my number. Okay?" he said, his dark eyes peering into hers.

Maria looked away. "Yeah, okay. Thanks. I will remember that."

Maria walked away, knowing she wouldn't need his help again. She'd never see him again, except in court maybe. Something inside Maria sank, but she ignored it, knowing she'd forget all about him once she moved back home.

CHAPTER FOUR

Derek called Maria to let her know that they questioned Trevor about information on the trafficking ring and even offered him a deal, but Trevor had not cooperated at all.

Unfortunately, CPDU still didn't know where the ring's headquarters was.

The next night, Maria and Carter packed everything they needed in bags and boxes. Relief covered her like the darkness that settled over the land.

Maria wanted to leave tonight. She'd been packing, selling her things, and planning to move ever since Trevor had found her.

She looked at her reflection in the bathroom mirror. She had bruises around her neck and on her face from when she hit the floor. There were more on her arms from when Trevor had pinned her to the floor. Her whole body was sore from defending herself.

The sooner she could leave, the better.

But first things first. Now that Trevor was no longer a threat, she could call her cousin Olivia and make amends. Maria dialed the number.

"Hello?"

"Liv? It's Maria."

"Maria? Oh, my goodness. How are you? I've missed you. How's Carter?" Olivia asked.

"We're doing well. Actually, that's why I'm calling. Trevor's been arrested. It's kind of a long story, but I actually broke up with him two years ago." Maria filled her cousin in on the details.

"I'm so glad you're free of him, Maria," Liv said. "Why didn't you call me sooner?"

"I didn't want to put you in danger. I figured you'd be safer if you didn't know where I was."

"I can take care of myself, Maria. You should have called me. I could have helped you."

"I should have listened to you when you warned me about him. You were totally right. You knew he'd be abusive and controlling, and I shut you out. If only I had listened to you…" Hot tears of regret stung Maria's eyes. She looked over at Carter. She could have protected him from so much if only she had listened to her cousin.

Maria paused, not sure how to say it. "Also, if I'm honest with myself, I didn't want to admit you were right. And that was wrong of me. I feel so stupid now."

"No. This isn't your fault. He targeted you. But I wish you would have let me help you. What are you going to do now?" Olivia said.

"Well, that's another reason why I'm calling. I'm moving back home."

"You're rejoining the Amish?"

"Yeah. I know this means we won't be able to speak again, because of the shunning…"

"If you think this is what is best for you and Carter, then you should do it. Don't worry about me, really."

"I just want him to have consistency. A better place to grow up," Maria said.

"It was a wonderful place to grow up." Sadness crept into Olivia's voice.

Maria had the feeling Olivia was remembering her deceased family who had died in a house fire at the hands of a sociopathic arsonist. Before that day, their childhood had been near perfect.

"Listen, Liv, I really am sorry for everything. For shutting you out."

"I forgive you, Maria. You're like a sister to me, forever and always."

"Forever and always."

"Can I see you before I go back to Unity?" Maria asked.

"I'm actually up in northern Maine investigating a case in the Amish community in Smyrna. Isaac is here with me too. CPDU temporarily transferred us. I wish I could see you, and I do wish you two the best. I'm so glad you're getting a fresh start," Olivia said, then she paused. "Oh, I'm actually about to start working now, so I have to go. I love you. It was so nice talking to you."

"I love you too. Tell Isaac I said hi. Bye, Liv."

45

They hung up, and Maria took in a cleansing breath, feeling a weight lift off her shoulders. Finally, after all this time, she was able to apologize to Olivia. It felt so freeing.

She went downstairs and leaned against the staircase railing, looked around the now empty house, and sighed. She had sold as much as she could the past few days, mostly at a pawn shop, and she'd also donated bags of items. She wouldn't need to take the large appliances with her, nor anything that would not be allowed into the Amish community. This small house was full of bad memories, and she couldn't sleep one more night there.

She knew her five-year-old son couldn't help with bigger boxes, so she made sure to pack things in smaller boxes and bags as well so he could feel more helpful than he was probably feeling. "Carter, help me carry the smaller bags to the car, please."

"Mommy, I don't want to right now," Carter complained. "I just want to play."

"Carter, do it now, please. I want to leave as soon as we can. Okay?"

"Okay." The boy reluctantly picked up a small bag and scurried out to the car.

The summer night air was warm as Maria put on the porch light and followed him with a box into the dim glow that semi-circled the side of the house. Darkness surrounded the rest of the property like an approaching enemy.

She shoved the box into the back of the car and heard a twig snap somewhere in the woods that surrounded the house. Her entire body tensed.

What was that? Her hand instinctively went to her gun. She slowly pulled it from its concealed holster on her hip.

Her heart launched into her throat and she froze, looking around like a frightened deer.

There it was again. A crunching branch somewhere in the trees.

It was probably a small animal. She was just paranoid, but she raised her weapon anyway.

"Carter, go back in the house. Right now," she commanded.

The little boy looked at her for a second, then his pudgy legs carried him swiftly into the little house. Maria followed him, then slammed the door and locked it. She leaned against it, her heart slamming against her rib cage.

Was someone out there?

She felt silly calling the cops over some weird noise in the woods that might very well be a squirrel or a raccoon. Derek's face entered her mind. He had said to call her if she needed anything at all…

Did this count? She could use help loading up all the boxes into her car, anyway, if it did end up being nothing. There was no way she and Carter could do all this in time tonight.

She scrolled down to his number in her phone and hesitated. Would he think she was silly for calling him over a snapping branch in the woods? Trevor was in jail. Who else would want to hurt her?

She wasn't sure, but there were plenty of sick people in this world. She called his number and waited as it rang. Her heart was pounding with nervousness. Would he take this the wrong way? As an excuse for him to come over?

"Agent Turner."

She swallowed. "Hi. It's Maria Mast. This is probably stupid, but I just heard a twig snap in the woods twice while I was loading up my car. It might just be an animal or something—"

She heard his car door slam. "I'm on my way."

"What? Are you sure? I mean, I don't want to bother you. Trevor is in jail, so maybe I'm just being paranoid."

"You're not being paranoid." She heard his car start over the phone. "He worked for the trafficking ring, so they might have someone from there watching you. I'll be there in a few minutes. Stay on the phone until I get there, okay?"

"Okay. Thanks."

"You still have that gun?"

"I'm holding it now."

"Good."

She peeked out the window. Could it really be someone from the sex trafficking ring watching her? Why would they do that? She didn't know anything.

But they didn't know that.

She checked on Carter, who was quietly playing with his farm animals on the floor. He looked up at her, eyes wide. "What's going on, Mommy? Why are you scared?"

"It's nothing, baby. It's okay."

"Why did you pull out your gun?"

"It's only a squirrel or raccoon that I heard, that's all."

"Then why did you call Agent Derek?"

"He's going to help us pack up."

Derek was still on the phone, and all she heard from his end was the hum of his engine. This was awkward. She hoped he would get here soon so that they could hang up.

A few minutes later Derek pulled into the driveway. She watched him, his gun drawn, flashlight beaming, looking into the woods. Then he hurried up to the house and Maria let him in.

"I didn't see anyone, but that doesn't mean they aren't there," he said, his frame filling the doorway.

"What should we do?"

"Let's wait in here a while and see what happens. If the prowler comes back again, I'll be ready to arrest them. If you leave, I might not get that chance again."

"I was hoping to go to Unity tonight, but that's okay. Safety is much more important." She looked back at Carter. "Whatever you think we should do. Thank you so much for coming."

"It's really not a problem, Ms. Mast. I told you to call anytime because I want to help in any way I can," he said, looking out the window.

"Call me Maria."

"Then you can call me Derek," he said, flashing her a charming grin.

She wrapped her arms around herself and looked away, ignoring the sudden spike in her pulse. "Look, we haven't eaten dinner yet. Are you hungry? We can eat while we wait this out."

"I wouldn't usually, but in this case and after smelling your food yesterday, I couldn't refuse that offer."

He had noticed her chicken parmesan? She couldn't help but blush a little, which she knew was ridiculous. She just smiled and turned around to start cooking. "I hope you like bacon alfredo."

"That sounds amazing," he said. "I'm a guy. I love bacon anything. Bacon pizza, bacon omelets, bacon ice cream..."

"Bacon ice cream?" Carter blurted, looking baffled.

"You've never had bacon ice cream, kid?" Derek pretended to be shocked by Carter's comment. "Or bacon donuts?"

Maria laughed out loud, something she hadn't done for as long as she could remember. "We've never even heard of that," she said, pulling things out of the bags of food and pots they had packed up.

"It actually is a real kind of ice cream, and bacon donuts are a thing too. I haven't been eating much besides microwavable meals or take out for a long time now. I really would appreciate a real meal," he said, going to look out the other windows and flipping on the rest of the outside lights.

"Why, your girlfriend can't cook?" The question slipped out, and she was grateful he couldn't see her clamp her hand over her mouth. She inwardly kicked herself for being so forward. It really wasn't her business, but she didn't see a ring on his left hand.

He dropped his voice low. "My wife passed away four years ago. She was a great cook, though."

She wanted to smack herself in the head. "I'm so sorry, Derek."

"It's okay, Maria. You didn't know," he said, his back still turned.

She shouldn't have even asked.

"I'm going upstairs to get a better look, okay?" he said, already going up the stairs.

"Sure. Whatever you have to do," she said, putting uncooked fettuccine into a boiling pot of water. She mixed up a homemade bacon alfredo sauce and added some bacon bits. Then she slathered some bread with butter, garlic, pesto and slid it in the oven.

After a few minutes, Derek came back down. "I don't see anything out there."

"Well, dinner is almost ready, so you can both sit down," she said.

"Let me help you set the table," Derek offered, taking the plates on the counter and putting them on the table. He took some cups from a box and laid them out along with some silverware.

She couldn't help but notice his tan, muscular arms again as he leaned over the table. She blinked rapidly and looked away, trying to ignore the heat rising in her face.

He was not even a friend to her yet. He was the agent assigned to her case. She meant nothing to him. She was a part of his job, and she'd be foolish and vain to think he considered her as anything more.

"Thanks," Maria said slowly.

Trevor had never once helped her set the table. It sure would be nice to be with someone like Derek. He seemed like a caring person, but it could have just been his professionalism.

Maria knew by now that a person could seem one way but have a completely different personality than what they showed.

"How are you feeling? You know, after what happened yesterday?" he asked.

"Physically or mentally?"

"Both."

"Sore and tired. Relieved that Trevor was arrested, but terribly sad those girls aren't any closer to being rescued."

"Really, you did all you could. Please don't feel bad."

Carter came running, and the three of them sat down at the table.

"After we pray, you can go up to the counter and take what you want. Do you mind if we pray?" Maria asked.

"We always thank God before we eat," Carter filled in.

"So do I," Derek said with a smile. "Well, I used to say thanks and I should more often."

Maria's eyebrows shot up a little at the surprise of Derek being a praying man. It was just so rare to meet one her own age these days. It was nice to know there were still some out there.

"Would you like to pray, Agent Derek?" Carter asked, folding his little hands together.

"Uh... Sure. Sorry. I haven't done this in a while," Derek stammered. He bent his head. "Dear Lord, we thank you for this fine meal Maria has made for us. Please keep this family safe and help this trip go smoothly for them. In Jesus' name, Amen."

"Good job," Carter said with a grin, giving Derek a thumbs up.

Derek laughed at the kid's good attitude. "Thanks, kid."

"Guests first," Maria said.

He took a heaping plate of the fettuccine and a large slice of garlic bread. "I'm starving," he muttered sheepishly. Once Maria and Carter sat down he took a huge bite, then another. "This is really good," he said around a mouthful of food.

"Thank you. I'm glad you like it," Maria said. Trevor had never complimented her cooking; he had only criticized it. But Derek seemed so hungry that he would probably think anything tasted good.

"So where are you from, Derek?" Maria asked.

"Savannah, Georgia originally," Derek said between bites. "Then my family moved up here when I was a kid."

"What's your family like?"

He smiled a little at the memory of his family. "My mother was Italian and my father was Irish. He grew up in Georgia. My mom was also a great cook, like you."

"Was?"

"My parents passed away ten years ago," Derek murmured, looking down at his plate.

"I'm sorry."

"Thanks. It was a long time ago."

"But I bet her Italian cooking was much better than this," Maria said.

"I'd say it's pretty close. Speaking of family—" Derek stood up and looked out all the windows again before sitting down. "So, your family is Amish?"

"Yeah. I have a cousin named Olivia who works at CPDU, but she is with her husband Isaac on a case in an Amish community up north right now. She's like a sister to me. We took her in when she was a teen after her entire family died in a fire. I just talked to her for the first time since before I left Trevor. He didn't like me talking to other people, especially family. So he made me stop talking to her when we were dating. For her own safety, I didn't contact her until he was arrested."

"Making you shut others out made you rely on him more. It's a control tactic," Derek blurted, but then caught Carter watching him, listening. "I'm sorry. So, what do you think about moving, Carter?"

"I'm excited," the little boy said cheerfully, his brown eyes widening. "This house is not very nice, and Mommy says her home is big. It has lots of farm animals. Farm animals are my favorite. I love farms," he chattered, grinning, poking at his food. "I love horses and pigs and cows and sheep and all animals. But especially farm animals."

"Wow," Derek said, laughing. Carter was energetic about what he liked. "I think you'll really like your new home, kid."

They finished up with dinner, and Maria started putting things away. "Let me help clean up," Derek said, gathering up the plates and bringing them to the sink.

"No, no, it's okay. You don't have to do that," Maria said, surprised by his kindness. She had asked him to come here to protect her, not to do dishes.

"I insist," he said, already filling up the sink with soapy water and pulling on her apron dramatically. He tried to pull on her hot pink rubber gloves, but his hands were too big so the gloves only went on half way.

He posed, putting his hands on his hips. "I'm actually pretty good at washing dishes," he said, wiggling his eyebrows. "You cooked, so let me clean."

Maria burst out laughing again at the sight of him in her pink gloves and apron. She didn't expect this agent to be so funny. He had seemed serious and unfeeling at first, but now she could see he had many more sides to him than his professional side.

"Thank you," was all she could say. The concept of a man doing dishes was completely new to her.

Growing up Amish, men never participated in kitchen chores. They were busy enough with milking cows, plowing fields or other types of outdoor work.

Trevor had never, ever done dishes or anything else to help her around the house.

Maria busied herself with packing the food away and putting it by the door to take home. Carter entertained himself again with his farm animals, and Derek finished quickly with the dishes. He looked out the windows again, removing the apron and gloves.

Maria peered out the front door window, and Derek was suddenly beside her, his movements too quick and silent for her to notice that he had gotten so close. "It looks like the coast is clear, but sometimes the most dangerous threats are unseen," he whispered above her ear.

Too close. She could smell his cologne and feel his body heat. He smelled wonderful, like a forest of evergreens and spring rain. She shied away, stepping back awkwardly, trying to control the redness spotting her cheeks.

"Do you think it's safe yet?" she stammered, pretending like she wasn't feeling anything.

He didn't seem to notice her awkwardness. "I'll go take a look around again. Wait here." He let himself out quietly and used a flashlight to scan the trees for any signs of movement. After circling the entire house, he returned. "Alright. We can start packing, but Carter needs to stay inside, and you need to listen to whatever I tell you. Okay?"

"Okay. It's probably nothing, as I said before. Sometimes I forget he's in jail, even though he was just arrested," she said quietly.

Sometimes she still feared that he would storm through the front door, attacking her in an angry rampage. Sometimes she thought she heard his diesel truck flying down the driveway.

She shuddered and turned to Carter, telling him to wait there. Then she grabbed some boxes with Derek and followed him out to the car, trying to ignore the way he looked in the moonlight.

It was too distracting. She told herself to just focus on packing quickly so they could get out of there.

And once she did, she doubted she would ever see Derek Turner again.

Yes, soon they would be in another town and surely he'd forget them as he was assigned another case. Something ached in her chest, but she ignored that too. She barely even knew this man. For all she knew, his true personality could be like Trevor's.

She had learned a long time ago not to trust anyone.

CHAPTER FIVE

Derek listened intently for any sounds coming from the woods, but all was silent tonight except Maria's soft breathing as she loaded boxes and bags into her car.

"There are some more bags in the house—" Maria began.

"Shh," he cut her off.

"What? Do you think it's—"

"Quiet!" he whispered fiercely, waving his hand. He could have sworn he had heard something. He looked into the shadows again, then the hair stood up on his arms and neck. Something didn't feel right.

"Get in the house," he whispered firmly.

Maria hesitated just a second too long.

There. Twigs crunched in the woods. His pulse lurched as he aimed his gun toward the direction of the sound, but he couldn't see anything. Was it an animal? If it was a prowler, the shadows concealed them all too well. Hopefully, Carter would stay inside the house.

Muffled popping sounds filled the air as bullets shattered and splintered the wood on the side of the house several feet away from them.

Derek covered Maria with his body, her small frame trembling beside him as she pulled her pistol from its concealed holster and he fired shots toward the direction of the shooter.

Derek ignored the way it felt to have Maria close to him. Instead, he snatched the flashlight from his belt and illuminated the shadows. He just wanted to protect her and Carter; that was all that occupied his mind.

He wanted to run to the woods and find the guy, but he couldn't leave Maria and Carter alone.

The unmistakable sound of footsteps met his ears, the sound dying as the trespasser ran deeper and deeper into the woods.

"Get inside now!" he ordered, and they both scrambled into the house.

"I think he's gone," Derek said once they were inside, still holding his Glock 21 pistol. "Are you okay?"

"I'm fine. Let me go find Carter," Maria said. She called for Carter, making sure he was okay. Derek figured the kid was probably hiding under the bed again. Derek would have done the same thing at five years old.

He looked outside the window at the trees, slightly moving the curtain aside. Either this prowler was an amateur or he was just trying to scare them, to show he was in control. He probably could have shot Derek or Maria if he had really wanted to, but instead he had shot the house several feet away from them.

Hopefully, Derek had scared the creep away. Either way, Derek didn't want to find out whether or not this guy would try to hurt Maria, or worse.

He called CPDU for backup and explained to Branson what had happened.

"I'll send backup, but the only person we have available is Agent Ben Banks. Everyone's already pulling double shift working the sex trafficking case. I can spare you Banks, but that's it," Branson told him.

Banks was still a relatively new agent and definitely not the best, but he would be better than nothing.

"I'll send him over now," Branson said.

"Thanks."

Derek hung up his phone and heard soft voices coming from upstairs. He waited until Maria came down.

"He's playing upstairs. He didn't realize that noise was gunshots. What... What just happened? Was that a silencer?" Maria asked, slowly stepping off the staircase, her hand brushing the railing, her blonde hair falling around her shoulders. "Who do you think that was?"

Derek stood near the door. Anger coursed through him at first, then the memory of finding Natalia dead in his own apartment made a wave of sorrow wash over him.

There was no way in this world that he would let these thugs hurt Maria. She was innocent, and she had been through enough already.

"Yes, it was a silencer. I think that whoever Trevor worked for is watching you or trying to scare you so you won't give the police information about the sex trafficking ring," he told her bluntly. "Since you dated one of their guys."

"But I don't know anything about it," Maria countered, sitting in a chair at the table. "I left him two years ago. Trevor never told me anything about the ring. I don't even know what it is called or where it is."

"But they don't know that. They might have some reason to believe Trevor told you secrets about the sex ring, secrets that might get them caught. Believe me, they will kill anyone for any reason they want to." He looked away, his dark eyes shrouded with what seemed like painful memories.

A few seconds passed silently, then Maria whispered, "Did traffickers kill your wife, Derek?"

He looked at her right in the eye. How had she known?

"Sorry. You just looked so sad when you said that," she said, nervously tucking a piece of golden-streaked hair behind her ear. "That was an absurd question."

"No, it's okay. You're right. They did," he admitted. He felt the sting of tears pricking his eyes, but he blinked the feeling away. "And we think this is the same trafficking ring that did it. We dealt with them four years ago and almost shut them down, but they got away. We did manage to put a few of them behind bars. I personally arrested one particular trafficker, and then his brother killed my wife for revenge."

Maria muttered something in what sounded like German. Then, she said softly, "I'm sorry. I can't believe people are capable of such horrible things. Where I am from, everyone helps one another. There is no violence. Well, at least there usually isn't. There was a killer on the loose at one point, but Olivia and Isaac caught him. That's a whole other story. Besides that one time, it's been peaceful and safe."

"That sounds like a perfect world." Derek envied her sheltered upbringing.

He had great parents, but some of the areas of his hometown had not been so peachy. Gunshots had not been a foreign sound to him when he was a child. As for Maria, he didn't want her to leave this house unprotected.

"I'm going to call my boss at CPDU and ask him to let me go to Unity with you as your bodyguard and stay until I arrest the perpetrator," Derek announced. "I can't let you leave town with this sociopath following you. Even if he is just trying to scare you."

"What? Are you serious?" Maria laughed. "I'm planning on joining the Amish again. You can't show up in your fancy car with your gun and expect the Amish to be fine with a policeman living amongst them. They don't cooperate with police. They don't believe in even asking the police for help or protection. For example, when an arsonist killed my cousin Olivia's family, the elders told her to not report it. They believe in leaving vengeance to God rather than seeking justice through law enforcement. If you want to come, you'll have to blend in. You'll stick out like a cow in a herd of horses."

Derek wanted to chuckle at her analogy about the cow, but she had a point. He couldn't march in there with his guns, flashing his badge, and expect the Amish to go along with it.

"Fine. You're right. That's what I'll have to do."

"What will the community think? What if they don't want you there?"

"Honestly, I don't really care what they think or if they want me there or not. I have to protect you and they can deal with it."

"The main thing is that you need to blend in. Will you be able to do that?"

"You'll have to help me."

"Of course."

"Good." He stood up, whipping out his cell phone. "Just give me a minute." He dialed his boss's number and waited, walking into the other room.

"Branson here."

"It's Derek again. I am worried someone either is trying to scare Ms. Mast out of giving us information she doesn't have, or they are going to keep watching her to make sure she doesn't."

"Wait a minute. Do you think there is a chance that Maria knows something but isn't telling us?" Branson asked.

"I don't think so, but maybe." Derek glanced at Maria in the other room, who was packing away a few more things. Her hair cascaded as she leaned over.

There was no way she would keep secrets about the trafficking ring, would she? In order to protect her ex-boyfriend?

What if she really was withholding vital information?

"We need to find out if she knows anything. It's possible she was threatened and is withholding information, or maybe she knows something without realizing it. Listen, Turner, if this trafficking ring stuff brings up too many bad memories about your wife, I understand—"

"No, I'm fine. I'd like to personally protect Maria. I mean Ms. Mast, sir. She's moving to her hometown in Unity, and I'd like to go with her. She's rejoining the Amish. She grew up Amish. I'll have to blend in with the Amish."

"I know she grew up Amish, just like her cousin Olivia did. They're sisters. Well, technically, they're cousins." Branson let out a laugh. "Wait. You, wearing suspenders, milking a cow? This I've got to see."

"Come on, Branson. I'd really like to go. Please give me this assignment." Derek rolled his eyes, shaking his head. If Branson ever saw him in his Amish getup, Derek would never hear the end of it.

Branson let out a deep breath. "It's the fourth anniversary of your wife's death this month. Can you really protect this woman, Turner? Considering the circumstances?"

Natalia's beautiful face flashed in his mind, with her dark eyes and long, dark hair. She had been his whole world.

"I can do it. It's my job. It won't get personal," he stated. They continued to discuss the details of the assignment.

"Fine, but Banks will go with you. It'll just have to be the two of you because we can't spare anyone else right now," Branson said in his deep, scratchy voice several minutes later. "I'll call Banks and let him know. Drive up to Unity in the same car as her, never leaving her side. Banks can go in a second car. If we get to the bottom of this, then we might get a lot closer to shutting down this sex trafficking ring."

There was nothing that Derek wanted more than to see that happen. He wanted justice for the girls who had survived being taken by these monsters. He wanted to see all those horrible men arrested. It wouldn't end human trafficking. Not even close. But it would be worth it if even one girl was rescued.

Derek put down his phone, walked into the kitchen and looked at Maria.

She stopped what she was doing and asked, "What is it?"

"So, my boss told me to go with you as your bodyguard. My colleague, Agent Banks, will also be coming to Unity."

Maria nodded. "Okay."

"Well, that's settled. Is it okay if I drive up to Unity with you in your car? Banks will go in a second car. Captain Branson told me to never leave your side."

"Yeah. Sure. I've got a lot to teach you about the Amish on the way there. But don't worry. They won't expect you to know everything about our ways," she said, going up the stairs to get Carter.

Derek smiled. "Good. I learn fast."

Maria gave him a sarcastic-looking smile and disappeared up the steps. He chuckled at her expression. She was incredibly composed considering the circumstances. Not to mention kind of funny, even though she wasn't trying to be.

She came back down with Carter, and the doorbell rang a few minutes later. Derek looked out the window to see Ben Banks standing there. He opened the door.

"Hi, Banks. Thanks for coming."

Ben only nodded. He was a man of few words. He was tall and broad-shouldered with his brown hair cut into a military haircut, almost filling the doorway with his large frame. His dark eyes were soft as he stood there awkwardly.

"Come on in." Derek opened the door wider and Ben stepped inside. "Ms. Mast, this is Agent Ben Banks."

Maria stepped forward and they shook hands. "Nice to meet you. Thank you for coming."

"Just doing my job, ma'am," he said with another curt nod.

"Hi, I'm Carter." Carter stuck out his hand and Ben awkwardly shook it.

"Nice to meet you," Ben said.

"You know, I was just thinking," Maria said. "My family goes to bed pretty early and I don't want to just show up at night unexpected. I'd call, but of course they don't have a phone in their house. You need to pack, considering you have no idea how long you'll be in Unity. How about we sleep here tonight and leave in the morning?"

Derek shook his head. "We can't stay here tonight. It's not safe. I'll double check with CPDU, but we should move you to a safe house tonight if you don't want to leave until tomorrow." Derek texted the captain and made sure. "He said yes. We can use it."

"Okay." Maria nodded slowly. "If you want, you should go to your place and get your things tonight for the trip to Unity."

"We can go on the way to the safe house," Derek said.

Maria turned to Ben. "What about you, Agent Banks? Do you need to go home and pack for the trip to Unity?"

"Our captain informed me so I'm already packed. I don't need anything."

"Okay. Want to take a ride in my unmarked police car, Carter? It doesn't look like a police car on the outside, but it does on the inside," Derek said.

"Yeah," the little boy squealed. "I love police cars!"

After Maria packed a bag for herself and Carter for the night, they locked up the house. They put Carter's car seat in the car and everyone got in the vehicle except Ben, who drove ahead of them.

"Here's the siren and that button is for the lights," Derek said, pointing to the blue lights that were off. Carter was fascinated by all the buttons and gadgets in the car. He fidgeted, pointing and asking questions and looking around with wide eyes.

"Can we turn on the lights?" Carter bounced on his car seat.

"I don't want to make a scene here in front of the neighbors, but how about if I turn them on for a second if no cars are around?"

"Yeah," Carter agreed, and they pulled out of the driveway.

Carter watched the cars on the road pass patiently. They drove along a long stretch of road. "There are no cars here!"

"Okay. Press this button," Derek said, showing him.

Carter pressed it, and his face lit up even brighter than the flashing lights. "Wow!" he cried.

Maria laughed as though she hadn't seen her son this happy and excited about something for a long time. She ruffled his hair lovingly, but he was so entranced he didn't seem to notice. "Pretty cool, huh?"

"When I grow up, I want to be a police officer," Carter declared.

"I thought you wanted to be a farmer." Maria laughed, the fear and terror she had felt only minutes earlier slowly melting away.

"Um… Maybe I'll do both."

"You're ambitious, kid," Derek said, glancing at Maria. She caught his smile, and she smiled back. Trevor had never made Carter so happy, not even when Maria had first started dating him and Trevor had seemed charming. Sure, Trevor had bought Carter gifts, but these were the types of things that really interested Carter and made him smile.

Gratitude swelled up inside her for Derek making her son giddy and for taking her mind off the lurker in the woods.

Or was she feeling something else?

No, it was gratitude. Nothing more. She appreciated how he made Carter smile and how he was protecting and helping them. That was all.

But she had to admit that things would be easier if he weren't so good-looking.

Derek turned off the blue lights, and they pulled into a parking lot a few minutes later. He led them up to his apartment. It was white, modern, and spacious—not to mention clean.

"Wow. This place is really nice," Maria said, admiring the spacious kitchen. She'd love to cook a good meal there rather than in her own tiny kitchen.

"Thanks. I basically only sleep here. I spend most of my time at work," he said, disappearing into his bedroom.

Carter looked out the window at the street below while Maria walked toward framed photographs on a shelf. She smiled at pictures of young Derek and pictures of who must have been his parents. She stopped when she saw a group of photos of Derek with a beautiful young woman.

His late wife.

The woman had long, dark hair and a wonderful smile. She looked like a genuinely kind person. Derek must have loved her very much. In the photo, he had his arms wrapped around her.

She hoped one day she'd have true love like that again and that it wouldn't be ripped away from her again like it had been for Derek. She had shared that kind of love with her late husband, Robert, until he had been killed. Their love had been true and rare, the kind that only came once in a lifetime. She doubted she'd ever feel that way about someone again.

CHAPTER SIX

In the bedroom, Derek shoved clothing and toiletries into a duffel bag. There was nothing for him to do here except feel alone. He preferred throwing himself into his work.

He had moved from his old apartment not long after Natalia's death. The memory of her lying dead on the floor had haunted him too much to stay there any longer, and he had never been able to fully get the stain from her blood out of the carpet. Now he had this apartment, but it just seemed empty.

He packed plenty of extra bullets, a flashlight, and his guns. His Glock 21, his HK45, and his good old Smith and Wesson Governor were his choice weapons. He grabbed pepper spray for Maria. Even though she had a gun, it would still be good for her to have pepper spray too. He always carried several weapons on him or had them near him at all times.

He left the bedroom and walked up to Maria, placing pepper spray into her hand.

"Here. You need to keep this on you at all times," he said quietly. "You just aim, turn the nozzle in the right position and spray. Doesn't cause any permanent damage, but it sure can bring down an attacker.

We all had to get sprayed with it during CPDU training. It hurts like crazy."

Maria cringed. "That sounds horrible. But I know how to use pepper spray. I already have some."

"Then keep this as an extra."

Maria's eyes wandered away, and he followed her gaze. He realized what she had been looking at: a photo of him and his wife.

"She was beautiful," Maria murmured.

Grief constricted his heart once again, and he let his eyes linger on the photo. He still missed her even four years later. He didn't think he could ever stop missing her. People told him it would get easier with time, and it had some, but he was not fully healed yet.

"Thanks. She was Russian. Very beautiful on the inside as well as the outside," he whispered. Then, he realized how close he was standing next to Maria. Suddenly it felt wrong with Natalia's picture right in front of them. Ignoring the questions bouncing in his brain, he turned away. "Okay, let's get going," he announced awkwardly, and mother and son followed him back to his car.

Once everyone was buckled in and they were on the road, Derek asked Maria, "Have you told him? About the plan?"

"Told me what?" Carter asked, sitting in the backseat.

Maria sighed, shaking her head. "Carter, when we go to Unity, it won't be as we first planned it."

"What do you mean? Will there still be farm animals?" Carter asked, concern lining his face, his brown eyes wide.

"Of course. There will still be farms and fields, and it will look like I described it to you. What I meant was Derek will be coming with us when we go back."

"That's great," Carter said, grinning. "To protect us from the man in the woods?" Carter asked softly.

"Yes. I'm not going to lie to you. I'm sorry you had to see that, but we are trying to make sure that doesn't happen again. That's why Derek is coming with us, to protect us."

"Why was that man in our woods? Does he want to get us?" Carter demanded. His face reddened, and his breathing sped up. He was about to cry. Carter hardly ever cried; it only happened when he was truly scared or sad.

"Carter, listen to me." Derek gripped the steering wheel tighter than necessary. "I'm not going to let anything bad happen to you or your mother. I promise. You have nothing to worry about. I'm very good at protecting people. It's what I do best. Okay?"

Maria stared at Derek as he drove, watched as he glanced at Carter in his rear view mirror. Derek obviously meant what he said, but should he really be making promises about things that he couldn't completely control?

She was about to put a hand on Derek's shoulder and tell him not to make such an extravagant promise, but she stopped when she saw Carter's face.

"Okay, Derek. You must be a hero." Carter beamed at the agent, finally settling back in his car seat, a look of relief and admiration washing over him.

But Maria knew that sometimes even people as strong as Derek couldn't prevent the worst from happening.

"No, kid. I'm no hero. Just doing my job," Derek's deep voice grumbled.

Derek and Ben took several winding turns as they drove in order to make sure they weren't being followed. They arrived once Derek was satisfied no one was tailing them.

Derek finally said, "Here we are. This is the safe house."

They drove up to a simple one-story white house that blended in with the other houses on the street.

A few minutes later, inside the house, Ben gave Maria a quick tour and took Carter to look around the rest of the house.

"Banks and I will take turns keeping watch, so one of us will always be on guard," Derek explained to Maria.

"Won't you be really tired?"

"Trust me. Banks and I can still do our jobs," he said, turning away. "In Iraq, sometimes we didn't sleep for days."

"Why?" she blurted, then wondered why she was prying.

"Well, Banks was in another platoon, so I don't know how it was for him. In Iraq sometimes my platoon slept on the ground in the desert; sometimes we had tiny mattresses we used to fight over." A sorrowful look crossed his face. "Sometimes we were on patrol for several days, so I didn't always get much sleep. We're trained to still be able to do our jobs even without sleep. Don't worry about us."

"What branch of the military were you in?"

"Marines. Banks was too. Almost everyone at CPDU has been or is in the military."

She wanted to ask him so many more questions. She wondered what places he had been sent to and if he had hated it or not. Her mind spun with questions. Had he lost any friends there? Were some things just too hard for him to forget? Did he duck every time he heard something that sounded similar to gunfire, like fireworks?

Now was not the time or place to ask. Maybe one day she would have the courage to ask him about it.

She caught herself. She barely knew this man. Why would she want to have that kind of a heart-to-heart conversation with him?

"The Amish are against war and violence, and they don't allow their church members to join the military," Maria said. "But I appreciate everyone who has served. Thank you."

Just say goodnight and walk to your room, she told herself.

He smiled at her and nodded in appreciation.

"Okay, well, I should get Carter to bed. Goodnight," Maria said.

"Goodnight," Derek said and watched her walk away.

She could feel his eyes on her back, and she made herself not run to her room.

As she helped Carter get ready for bed she told herself to stop acting silly and being personal with Derek. She had to stop whatever feelings were surfacing within her whenever she looked at him. But she couldn't help it. His dark gelled hair, angled jaw, short beard and those dark eyes made him handsome. She knew that was all it was, that and the fact that he was her bodyguard. He made her feel safe. She wasn't sixteen anymore, but she sure felt like it.

She tucked Carter into bed and kissed him on the forehead.

"I like Derek and Ben Banks," Carter said sleepily.

"They are nice, huh?"

"Yeah... A lot nicer than Trevor. Especially Derek. He saved you from that bad man."

Pain stabbed her core. Of course Carter loved Derek. He was twice the man Trevor would ever be; he was a hero in the boy's eyes. Another pang hit her heart when she realized Carter would most likely start to see Derek as a father figure and friend. He'd become attached.

What would happen when Derek walked out of their lives forever and went back to his job while they stayed in Unity?

***

As Ben kept watch, Derek drifted between being asleep and awake. The remnants of a dream floated through his mind. His friend Danny stood beside him in Iraq. The scent of dusty sand and blood filled the air. One moment Danny was standing there beside Derek, and suddenly bullets peppered the air. Derek ducked back around the building as Danny was hit, blood soaking his gear. Derek watched helplessly behind a building like a coward as his friend died only a few feet away. He wanted to help and he wanted to reach out to him. But the more Derek reached, the farther away Danny seemed to be.

"Turner! Wake up!" Ben shook him awake. "Someone's out there."

Derek's eyes shot open.

He grabbed his 9mm M&P Shield, and they sprang toward the door as a shadow outside moved across the window near the front door. Derek stood near the door and listened, then opened the door a crack. Footsteps hurried around the other side of the house. He opened the door and swept the area with his gun, Ben right behind him.

No one was in sight.

Derek motioned for Ben to go around the back, and Ben took off running around to the other side of the house.

Derek listened a moment more, then dashed into the house to look out the window that was on the other side of the house. He saw a dark figure darting across the yard, headed for a cluster of trees and bushes. Derek bolted out the back door to see Ben chasing after the prowler, but the man was far ahead of Ben. There was no way Ben would catch up. Derek stayed in the house in case there was a second prowler.

A few minutes later, Ben came back to the house, completely out of breath.

"Did you see him?" Derek asked.

"Couldn't see his face. He was fast and he had a head start."

Great.

"What's going on? I heard something."

Derek whipped around to see Maria coming down the hall, her hair somewhat mussed in an endearing way.

"Everything is okay. We saw someone at the door, but he ran off."

"Did you see who it was?"

"We didn't see his face."

"All that matters is that we are safe for now," Maria said softly and padded back down the hall in her slippers.

Derek wouldn't use the word safe, but at least they were all still alive.

CHAPTER SEVEN

In the morning, Maria awoke to the realization that everyone in the house was okay. Nothing else had happened. Maybe the stalker had been scared off for good.

And maybe elephants could fly.

Maria shivered, squeezing her eyes shut, praying the prowler would never return. Miraculously, she had fallen asleep after the ordeal last night and had peacefully slept until morning.

Or maybe it had been Derek himself. His presence in the house had calmed her.

No. She denied that notion instantly. She knew what had calmed her: prayer. After returning to her room, she had begged God to protect the safe house from any danger. Once again, God had shown Himself faithful to her.

Everyone was alive and there was no sign of the trespasser. Feeling optimistic, Maria quickly dressed, checked on Carter and went to the kitchen to make breakfast.

She crept down the hall, trying not to wake up whichever man was sleeping. She peeked her head around the wall and saw Banks sprawled out crookedly on the couch.

She took another step and the floorboards beneath her let out a high-pitched creak. She winced. But Banks didn't move.

Derek stood by the window in the kitchen. "Good morning."

"Good morning. Did anything else happen last night?"

"Nothing except for Banks' snoring."

"That's a relief. I'm going to make breakfast. Did you sleep at all?" she asked, going into the kitchen and putting two pieces of bread in the toaster.

"I slept for a bit while Banks kept watch."

Carter came into the kitchen wearing puppy pajamas, scratching his head of unruly hair.

"Good morning, sunshine," Maria said.

He rubbed his eyes and sat down to eat toast at the table.

"I'll make you some toast, too," Maria said to Derek.

"Thanks," Derek said, sitting where Maria gestured. "I usually don't even eat breakfast."

"Well, that's not good for you," Carter remarked, now more awake. "Breakfast is the most important meal of the day."

"Get used to breakfast. In Unity, the Amish always have big breakfasts, usually with a lot of variety," Maria said.

Derek smiled. "I'm fine with that. Do they ever cook bacon?"

"Sometimes," Maria said with a laugh. "But there are usually lots of sausages, eggs, and fruit at breakfast. Pancakes, too."

"I love pancakes!" Carter chimed in. "Especially with chocolate chips."

"Sometimes they even eat cookies at breakfast."

"Cookies for breakfast?" Carter gasped.

"No way. I think I'll like it in Unity," Derek said with a grin.

Banks woke up and silently ate his breakfast, only muttering a thank you to Maria when she handed him a plate of toast. Derek helped clean up once again, even though it only took a few minutes.

"You know, Amish men don't help in the kitchen. They go right to work or do their chores after they finish eating and the women clean up. You really need to stop doing this," Maria pointed out.

"Well, fine then. We aren't in Unity yet. Just let me enjoy my last breakfast clean-up in peace," Derek said, drying the dishes they had washed.

"Well, thanks for the help, then," Maria said.

"You're welcome. I doubt that the man will return now that it is daylight, so I won't have a chance of arresting him. We can leave. I just need to go outside and look over your vehicle while Banks stays in here with you."

"Why?"

"I need to check for tracking devices. You and Carter stay here in the house with Banks."

"Oh. Okay. I'll go finish up a few things."

After eating, Maria went up to her room and packed up the few belongings she'd brought. She stuffed her toothbrush and shampoo in a backpack along with a few other things.

Maria clipped her holster to the waist of her jeans, slipped her gun in and pulled her long shirt over it to conceal it.

***

Outside, Derek inspected Maria's vehicle for tracking devices. After a few minutes, he found what he was looking for under the car. It was two old transistor radio-sized boxes. One was the transmitter, and the other one held batteries. Both had been attached to a metal section under the car with magnets. He put on a pair of gloves and removed the device.

He brought it inside and checked it for prints with Ben, but it had been wiped clean.

They finished packing up a few more things into the cars, then left for Unity. Derek arranged for someone to pick up his car and the tracking device at Maria's house.

Maria glanced in the rear view mirror as she drove away, glad to be leaving all those horrible memories behind.

She looked forward to what was in store and the wonderful life she could build for her and Carter. Finally, he'd have some stability in his life and a real future.

***

Derek checked the rearview mirrors every few seconds as he rode in the passenger seat of Maria's car. Ben drove ahead of them in his car.

With an uneasy feeling that would not rest, Derek couldn't be too careful as he watched for someone following them.

His eyes darted back and forth to the mirror as they drove along a long stretch of a tree-lined backroad.

"There's no one even on this road. Don't worry," Maria said.

But he did worry. It was his job to worry. But he leaned back a little farther into his seat and relaxed his tense muscles a fraction. Maybe they really had left with no one knowing where they were going.

"So, do you still carry your…piece?" Derek asked, glancing at her, then Carter.

"He knows what a gun is and that I carry one. I teach him gun safety, and he knows he should never touch one. I was carrying mine, but now that I'm joining the Amish, I'm not sure if I will keep doing it."

"What? Why not?"

"The Amish in Unity only use guns for hunting. We aren't allowed to carry them for self-defense," she explained.

"Come on, Maria, your circumstances are different," he said, clearly trying to choose his words carefully in front of Carter. "I think in your case it would be okay if you break the rules. Who has to know? It's concealed."

"I hate lying. Besides, I'd be shunned if they found out after I officially rejoined the church. I don't want to be shunned again. You have no idea what that's like, to be cut off from family."

"Actually…" Derek began.

"I'm sorry. I shouldn't have said that," Maria said, regret lacing her words. "I'm just not sure what I should do yet."

"Well, then think about it. It could save your life." Derek understood that she didn't want to mess up her second chance, but it wouldn't be worth it if she ended up dead. Carrying a gun could save her life.

"So, you want to know more about the Amish?" Maria asked as she drove.

"That would be a good idea. I really don't know much about them at all except that they dress weird. No offense."

Maria smiled a little. "Well, we're very traditional. We don't dress in modern clothing or use modern technology because the Bible says to be content with what you have. Though, some of the houses do have outlets in the basement for charging battery-operated things. We use battery-operated lanterns instead of kerosene lamps. They are a lot safer.

"We call people who are not Amish *Englishers* and things that are modern *English*. We learn Pennsylvania Dutch before we learn

English, which we learn when we go to school. Instruments are forbidden. We don't comment on each other's looks. Oh, and in church, don't be surprised if you see men kiss other men and women kiss other women."

"What?" Derek blurted.

"In the Bible it says to greet each other with a holy kiss. Also, the women and men sit on separate sides of the room during church. The service is in Pennsylvania Dutch and English. Some communities hold church in members' homes, but we have our own church building. Some communities have it every other week, but we have it every week. Three hours and one and a half hours, alternating weeks."

"Three hours for church?"

Maria laughed. "I'm sorry to say you won't understand a good part of it."

"Oh, fun."

"And don't worry—other than the sermons, they will speak English around you to be polite. You'll understand what's being said."

"Okay, good."

"And weddings. I know ours are different than what you are used to. The bride and groom don't kiss at the wedding, and there's no white dress or cake or anything fancy like that. It is actually similar to a regular three-hour church service."

If Derek ever did get married again, he wouldn't care too much about what his wedding day would be like, but he sure was glad the ceremony wouldn't be three hours long. And no kiss? He preferred *Englisher* weddings, thank you very much.

"Anyway, that's not really important because you probably won't be attending a wedding," Maria said. "Amish men who are married have beards and Amish men who are single have no facial hair, but Amish men never have mustaches. But you don't have to shave if you don't want to because you're not Amish. We don't except *Englishers* who visit to follow our rules. We aren't easily offended, so don't worry about that," Maria told him. "I might have clothes at my parents' house that you can borrow that will help you look like an Amish man. If not, you can borrow my father's or someone else's."

He scrubbed a hand over his short beard. "Whatever helps me blend in the most."

Only a few minutes later, Derek looked into the rearview mirror to see a white truck with no license plate speeding up behind them. Fully alert, he gripped his gun. Was this just some stupid driver about to pass them or was this the man who had been watching them from the woods? Derek couldn't see the driver because the truck was higher than them and the windows were tinted.

The roar of the engine behind them answered his question. The truck rear-ended them, the slamming impact sending them all lurching forward in their seats. Carter cried out in fear.

"Get down!" Derek yelled.

He threw himself onto the backseat behind Maria and rolled down the window. He aimed for the truck's tires and fired, but missed as the truck accelerated. The other vehicle pulled up beside them on the driver's side, then slammed into the side of their car, making the car almost careen off the side of the road. Derek dropped his gun during the impact.

Carter cried out again.

Derek called Ben, who he had on speed dial. "Let us go by. Try to pull him over and arrest him."

"Copy that," Ben said and hung up.

"Drive past Ben," Derek told Maria. She hunched down as she drove, praying quietly. Carter bent forward, covering his face with his hands. Derek aimed and fired at the truck again, hitting the front bumper instead of the tires as Maria's car sped forward.

Ben switched on his red and blue lights and let Maria drive past him. She flew past Ben's car.

"Keep going. We need to get as far away from that truck as possible. Ben will take care of it. You both all right?" Derek asked, turning to Carter and running a hand over his hair.

Maria only nodded, tears threatening. She blinked them away. "Carter?"

"I'm okay," he squeaked. He clutched his toy horse so hard that his little knuckles were white. He slowly sat back up. "Was that the bad man?"

"Well, I think so. There is a slight chance it was just a crazed drunk driver with road rage. But remember what I promised? I didn't let him hurt you," Derek said.

Maria looked at Derek in the rearview mirror as he said the words. Derek could see gratitude in her eyes, but he also saw fear.

She locked her eyes back on the road and trembled. Derek climbed ungracefully back onto the front seat, then instinctively reached out and covered her right hand with his.

"It's okay," he whispered.

She jumped slightly, then kept her expression unreadable as she continued to focus on the road. He drew his hand back, embarrassed.

He did it again. He had gone too far. It was his job to protect Maria, not comfort her when she was scared. He turned to look out the window, hoping he hadn't offended her.

***

Maria tried to act unaffected as Derek took his hand off hers. The simple gesture had been meant to calm her down. Instead, it made her uneasy, sending sparks up her arm, shooting straight for her heart. Derek was gentle, thoughtful, helpful, and good with Carter… And he made her feel safe for the first time in so long.

She could see him staring out the window from the corner of her eye as he called Ben, then his captain to inform him of the attack.

Derek was just doing his job. He probably was like this with all of the people he protected.

Derek hung up the phone. "Ben went after the truck, but there was a passenger inside. They shot out Ben's tire and got away." He slammed the dashboard. "We could have had him."

They stopped at a car repair shop to get a new tire for Ben's vehicle, changed his tire, then kept driving. As Maria drove closer and closer to her childhood home, anxiety churned in her stomach, despite the familiar sights of farmland and the neighbors' houses.

Maybe she should have called her father's cabinet shop phone first instead of showing up unannounced like this. The Amish didn't have phones in their houses, but they did in their businesses along with shared community phones.

She could have probably reached them in time. But if Maria was honest with herself, she had been too afraid to call.

How would her family react to seeing her? Would they want her back after all the choices she had made? Would they love Carter?

Joy eclipsed her anxiety as she thought of how happy it would make Carter to meet his grandparents for the first time and how excited he would be to see the farm animals.

And how would they react to Derek and her situation?

Before she could plan out what she was going to say to her parents in her head, they were driving down the long dirt road that led to her home. The same horses still roamed the fields; chickens still clucked in the barnyard. Mary Mast's garden was in full bloom, colored with summer flowers of many colors like black-eyed Susans and roses. Even the raspberry bushes were plentiful.

She opened the car door and deeply inhaled the scent of grass, fresh air, and her mother's flowers. It was absolutely heavenly. She never realized how much she had missed it until now.

"Horses! Chickens!" Carter squealed, jumping out of the car, making a beeline for the animals. Ben pulled up in his car and got out.

Derek chuckled as he started lifting bags out of the trunk. "I think Carter will learn to like this place." Ben came over to help with the bags.

Maria hefted two bags onto her shoulders and made her way up the stairs to the front porch, feeling as if with every step the bags weighed another ten pounds.

When she reached the door, she stared at it hesitantly before knocking, remembering how her parents had looked at her when they had learned she intended on leaving with an outsider.

Maria knew it had hurt them so much more than it had hurt her. She would never fully understand how much it had hurt them, losing both of their daughters to the outside world.

Before she could change her mind, she knocked on the front door. Soft footsteps sounded. The door opened to reveal her mother. Mary Mast had a few more wrinkles and a few more gray streaks in her hair. She was still as lovely as ever with her delicate features and dancing green eyes that now filled with what Maria hoped were tears of joy.

Mary hesitated, clearly remembering that Maria was shunned and could not be spoken to unless she was going to repent and rejoin the Amish faith, which she was.

"I've come home, *Maam*. For good. I want to repent and rejoin the church. If you will have me."

"Of course, Maria!" Mary cried out, letting out a sob. She threw her worn hands around Maria in a motherly bear hug.

Warmth and relief flooded Maria.

"I missed you so much, my baby," Mary whispered into Maria's hair. "You will never know how much."

Maria wiped away her own tears. "I missed you, too. Both of you. Where is *Daed*?"

"Your father is at the cabinet shop, but he is coming home for an early lunch soon. Come in, come in!" Mary said excitedly, then finally noticed Derek and Ben. Derek was coming up the steps while Ben stood by Carter, who was still playing with the chickens. "Hello, there," Mary said to Derek.

"Hi, my name is Derek Turner," Derek said, offering his hand to shake, then withdrew. He must have remembered how Maria had told him Amish women in Unity do not shake hands with men.

"It's nice to meet you, Derek. I'm Maria's mother, Mary. Gideon, her father, is coming home from work soon for his break. He works just down the lane."

Carter ran up the steps and looked up at Mary while Ben got more bags from the cars. "Hi," Carter said, a little out of breath from running around the yard.

New, unshaped tears filled Mary's eyes. "This must be Carter," she said, her voice cracking with emotion when she said her grandson's name. He nodded energetically, then Mary knelt and hugged him tightly.

"Hi, Carter. I'm Mary, your grandmother."

"You're my grandmother?" Carter asked in a small voice. When Mary nodded, Carter flung his arms around her waist, and Mary's tears finally fell.

"I'm so glad to meet you, Carter. I've waited a long time for this," she told him softly. Maria watched, her heart full of contentment and gratitude. She caught Derek watching her, a crooked smile on his face. He immediately looked away.

Had he been admiring her, watching her? Her own embarrassment covered her face. Maybe she had been wrong. He had only known her for a short time. She would be vain for thinking that he had feelings for her already or that he thought she was beautiful. She shooed away the thoughts, then went inside the house along with Carter, Mary and Derek.

***

Derek followed Mary inside the house.

"Are you two dating, or—?" Mary asked, looking from Derek to Maria. Carter moseyed around the kitchen, gaping at the wood stove.

"No," they both blurted out.

Derek didn't even dare look at Maria after the incident that had just occurred. She had caught him staring at her. He had been admiring how the sun brought out the gold highlights in her hair, how her eyes had watered at the sight of her son meeting his grandmother for the first time. It had been a perfect moment until he had ruined it with his awkwardness.

One would think a trained field agent would be stealthier, smoother. When Maria was around him, he seemed to forget everything he had ever been taught about hiding his emotions.

"We aren't dating," Derek stated.

There was a knock on the door. Derek looked out the window. "It's just Ben."

Mary let him in.

Derek said, "Mrs. Mast, this is my partner, Ben Banks."

Ben set down the bags he had gotten out of the cars. "Nice to meet you, ma'am. We are doing everything we can to protect Maria and Carter."

"What do you mean?" Mary asked incredulously.

The front door opened and a man with a long gray beard stepped in, looking weary from a busy morning at work. He took one look at

Maria and called out her name happily, and she hurried over to him. He hugged her close and stroked her hair, tears of joy in his eyes.

"*Daed*," Maria murmured. "It's so good to see you. I'm here to stay. I'm home. I'm so sorry I left the way I did."

At her words, a new round of tears came, and her father held her face in his hands. "All is forgiven, Maria. Nothing would make me happier than to have my daughter home again. I missed you so much. This is so wonderful. Now that you are staying, you will no longer be shunned if you repent and rejoin the church."

That's it? Derek thought. They were ready to take her back just like that after all this time? He felt his own eyes sting a little with tears that he quickly blinked away.

"I am rejoining the church. I wanted to come home and raise my son in a loving, stable environment. Carter, come meet your grandfather." Carter ambled over and Maria's father pulled him into a hug, welcoming him.

Derek watched, happiness for the family filling him. Longing for his own family started to take over, edging its way in. But everyone he loved, his wife and family, were dead.

He would probably never know what it felt like to belong to a family again. His job took over his life, so he had no time for a girlfriend. He didn't plan on settling down anytime soon, anyway. That was fine with him.

Gideon suddenly noticed Derek standing there. "Who are these young men?"

"This is Agent Derek Turner and Agent Ben Banks. They are my bodyguards," Maria told him slowly. Gideon's eyes grew to the size of quarters as Ben and Derek both pulled out their CPDU badges.

"Please, call us Ben and Derek," Derek said. "We don't want to raise any unwanted attention."

"Wait... Bodyguards?" Gideon asked, squinting.

Mary's face paled. "What is going on here? Why do you need bodyguards, Maria?" she stammered.

By now Carter had wandered upstairs to look around so they could speak freely.

Derek explained, "Someone is trying to scare Maria into keeping quiet. The man she was dating, Trevor Monroe, was working for a human trafficking ring based out of Portland. I work for Covert Police Detectives Unit in Portland. We have been trying to locate and shut down the ring for a few years. We arrested Trevor, and someone seems to think Maria knows information about the ring, but she doesn't. I don't think they are trying to kill her. If they wanted her dead, then she probably would be. They might even want her alive so they can get her to tell them what she knows or if she has told anyone anything. Maria wanted to come back here, so I was assigned to protect her until I catch whoever is after her. Agent Banks was assigned to be my partner. We will stay out of your way, but our main goal is to make sure Maria and Carter stay safe and hopefully to arrest the perpetrator."

Mary let out a long breath, the color slowly returning to her face. "Lord, help us," she prayed, and Gideon patted her arm reassuringly. Then she asked Derek and Ben, "Do you think Maria is safe here?"

Ben nodded. "We think so. Trevor and the person after her—or people after her—probably have no idea she grew up Amish. This is the last place they'd think to look."

Derek added, "Is it all right if we stay here, in this house, so we can protect Maria as a precaution?"

"I don't know about this," Gideon said to Mary.

"Me neither. We usually open our home to whoever needs to stay here, but..." Mary's sentence trailed off.

"Look, I get it. We are two strangers who want to stay with you. You might be wondering if you can trust us, especially with your daughter. Let me assure you, we are ready to risk our lives to protect her. And in order to protect her, we need to be in the same house as her," Derek explained.

"I would not usually let a young man not married to my daughter stay in the same house as her, but under these circumstances, we need to do what is safest. Do you agree, Mary?" Gideon said.

"You're right. Yes, I agree. You can both stay in the spare room down the hall from ours."

"What should we say when people ask about you?" Gideon asked, then looked at Maria with eyes full of love. Derek could see that the man was clearly shaken but was hiding it well.

"I suppose we should just say we are friends. I don't think we should go around telling people we are Maria's bodyguards. It might cause people to panic. Don't you think so?" Ben asked, crossing his arms in front of him.

"No, the people here won't panic. I think it would be best to be honest with them. Then they could be on the lookout for a prowler. The Amish trust in God with every aspect of our lives. We do not panic during dangerous situations." Mary turned to Maria. "We will be supportive and alert during this time. We will fervently pray for your safety. This is the best place for you, my dear," Mary said, motherly love shining in her eyes.

"And as I said, of course you can stay in this house, but if I see you either of you trying anything on my daughter, misters..." he wagged his finger, staring Derek and Ben down.

"You don't have to worry about that, sir. We are here to protect her. That's what we intend to do."

Derek had said the words mostly to reassure himself why he was here. It certainly was not to enjoy the way her face lit up when her father had walked in, admire how good a mother she was to her son, or notice the way she tucked strands of hair behind her ear. That was not part of his job to notice those things. Those things shouldn't even be crossing his mind. Derek shouldn't feel revival in his heart when she looked him in the eye or when she smiled at him.

He turned to walk back toward Maria's car and park it in the woods where it would be hidden, just in case anyone did come looking for her, which he doubted.

He definitely did his job better with a heart of stone. That way he never got emotionally involved. More importantly, his heart wouldn't end up broken.

***

"Do you still have Robert's clothes and things?" Maria asked her mother softly as they brought their bags upstairs. "I hoped you'd keep at least some, even though I was gone so long."

"Actually, I always hoped you would come back, so I did keep them. I didn't feel right giving them away, and I wasn't sure what you wanted to do with them. They are in a chest in here," Mary said, entering Maria's tidy bedroom.

It looked just like she had left. The same intricate, colorful quilt Maria had made still covered the twin bed. The same simple nightstand stood beside the bed, near her solid wood dresser that her father had crafted with skilled, strong hands. A braided rug offered some warmth from the hardwood floors that became chilly in the winter months, providing some solace for her feet during trips to the bathroom at night.

There was no clutter, only simplicity and the bare necessities. Homemade, curtains framed the windows that displayed a perfect view: serene, green fields and tall grass blowing in the summer wind, dotted by wildflowers. The road to town was there, too, but was distant, just like her memories of her late husband.

"Have you heard from Freya again?" Maria asked, her voice cracking a bit.

Maria had been there that day Freya admitted to the family that she had been the one who accidentally killed Robert. Robert's parents readily forgave Freya.

Maria wouldn't lie. She didn't want to forgive the woman at first. But once Maria learned more about Freya, and the more she prayed about it, Maria realized she had to forgive the woman.

And once she did, her heart felt so much lighter. Now Freya was a family friend who visited every now and then. She was growing closer to Robert's brother, Adam, who had left the Amish right after Robert's death.

"Yes, actually. She's doing well, and so is Adam. She was here to visit a few weeks ago."

"That's good to hear."

Maria's heart had been blackened with anger, confusion, and pain after Robert died, especially before she knew who had killed him.

When Trevor had come along after she left home, she had eagerly let him kiss away her pain. Much too eagerly. Finally, the hurt had

100

subsided. She began to love again, blinded by Trevor's deceptive charm.

And look where that had gotten her.

But she had never lost her faith in the Lord.

Maria realized she had been staring at the chest for several minutes when her mother whispered, "I'll give you some privacy," and backed out of the room.

Maria knelt in front of the chest, running a hand over the woodwork. She lifted it open and peered inside. Robert's crisp, folded clothing sat in neat piles above his favorite books and sketchbooks of his fine drawings. She had sat with him under the big oak tree down the lane many times, watching him draw the horses or landscapes. Sometimes he would even draw her.

He had taught her how to draw, and Robert had often complimented her on how talented she was. She had continued to draw over the years, and not many people knew how talented she was. It was a secret that was dear to her heart. It helped her feel close to him, especially when she looked at the drawings he had helped her create.

Maria fanned through the pages and found a sketch Robert had done of her. She looked much younger; her long hair was tied up under a white *kapp*. She wore a colorless, plain frock, and a few wisps of hair framed her smiling face.

Maria had been so innocent and untainted then, unaware of the atrocities people committed on a daily basis to women like her.

She pulled out a button-down white cotton shirt, pants, suspenders and a soft black hat. Typical clothing for an Amish man. Some Amish communities didn't allow buttons on their clothing, but in Unity they wore them.

Maria lifted the garments to her nose and inhaled, but the scent of Robert had been masked by the wood smell of the chest over the years. She smoothed out the material on her lap, wondering how her life would have been if he had not been killed. How many children would she have by now? How trusting would she have been without enduring Trevor's abuse? Would she be more loving?

She opened the closet and put on a lavender frock, then tied up her long hair and put a white prayer *kapp* over it. Maria looked in the mirror, finally beginning to feel at home again.

The past was in the past, and there was no sense in reminiscing, not with someone trying to scare her into keeping quiet regarding a trafficking ring she knew nothing about. She had to think about keeping Carter safe. She had to stop thinking about Derek's expressive dark eyes and how she caught him watching her.

She definitely should not be thinking about that at all.

She prayed about continuing to carry her concealed weapon. Should she follow the Amish ways and have no way to protect herself?

Not always having her gun strapped to her under her clothing would take some getting used to.

It had been hard at first for her to go against her upbringing and carry the firearm, but now she was so used to always having it there, making her feel safer. More secure. Maria wondered what her parents would say if they knew she carried a gun.

She rose and brought the clothing downstairs to Derek.

Maria would have to decide what to do about the gun later.

CHAPTER EIGHT

As Mary finished preparing lunch, Maria went downstairs to the spare bedroom, dressed in a light purple dress and white bonnet-like head covering. Though the clothing was plain, and her hair was no longer flowing around her shoulders, she still looked beautiful. Maria stood in the hall outside the bedroom.

"Where is Ben?" she asked Derek, looking around.

"He's taking a walk around outside to make himself familiar with the property. I will go later," he explained, stepping out of the room to join her in the hallway.

"That was Olivia's old bedroom," she told Derek.

"She must have had a culture shock when she went out into the world after leaving this place."

"Well, Liv's family was killed by an arsonist and she was married to an abusive man for several years. So, her life here wasn't as peaceful as you might think. It's a long, complicated story. I imagine her life was much better after she left here. We both had terrible taste in men at one point." She wrinkled her nose. "Anyway, here's some clothing to help you and Ben blend in. The pants might be a bit short on you and Ben, but hopefully they are good enough. They were my husband's."

He looked up and caught her gaze when she handed him the clothes. She had mentioned at CPDU that Carter's father had passed away, but now several questions bounced around in Derek's head.

"He was killed in an accident shortly after we were married. I was pregnant with Carter. They never met," she explained.

"I'm sorry." This woman had survived more heartache than anyone else he knew.

"Thanks. It was a long time ago."

Seeing the grief in her eyes, he took the clothes. Clearly coming home had brought back old memories.

"Did you decide whether or not you're going to carry your gun?" he asked in a quiet voice.

Maria didn't answer at first, looking deep in thought. "I prayed about it, but I'm still not sure."

"Maria, you need to think of your own safety before the Amish rules. I know the rules are important to you, but this is a unique situation. Think about Carter. At least protect yourself for his sake. What about the pepper spray?"

She sighed. "If you really think I should, then I will carry both the pepper spray and the gun."

"Good. Thank you."

"Well, we are going to eat lunch if you want to come join us after you change. Oh, and there are outlets in the basement for you to use to charge your phone."

"Okay, thanks," he said. "Wait, there are outlets in this house? That's allowed?"

"Yes. We only have a few for charging battery-operated devices. It's run on solar power."

"That's surprising. I was also surprised that your parents are letting me stay here, even though they don't even know me," Derek said.

"Everyone here is very hospitable and trusting. It is the Amish way. Well, we will see you in the kitchen."

Questions still lingered in his mind as she walked down the hall. He went back in the bedroom and closed the door. He unfolded the white shirt, dark pants and suspenders. Branson would really laugh if he saw Derek in this outfit.

Derek changed into the simple clothing, looked in the mirror and adjusted his black-rimmed glasses. Luckily some of the Amish here wore glasses.

He smoothed down his dark, mussed hair and eyed the scruffiness of a beard on his square jaw. Maria had told him that Amish men did not wear mustaches, so he'd have to take care of that. He pulled out his toiletry bag and quickly shaved off his mustache, but he kept the rest of the short beard. To the eyes of a no-good, shooting thug who was after the woman he cared about, he would hopefully look like any other Amish man…unless of course these were the same thugs who had killed his wife and knew what he looked like.

The woman he cared about? Where had that thought come from? Maria was his assignment, not his friend, and certainly not anything more than that. He shook his head as if to clear it. *When did you get so careless and off your game?* he silently asked his reflection.

It had all started when this beautiful woman had stepped into his life, needing his protection. Well, that was all she was going to get, because after this stalker was caught, he would never see her again.

Derek ventured out into the kitchen. Gideon was playing a card game with Carter, and Maria was helping Mary prepare the meal. Mary set the table and Maria sliced freshly baked homemade bread with careful and slow movements. For a moment he let himself watch her, even started to admire the way that lavender dress looked on her, how the vertical folds in the fabric fell against the back of her ankles, then he forced himself to look away.

"Where would you like Ben and me to sit?" he asked.

At the sound of his voice, Maria looked up and stopped what she was doing. A smile tugged up the corners of her mouth as she looked him up and down. Then she seemed to catch herself. She turned back around and continued with her task.

He looked down at himself. Was she trying not to laugh at how ridiculous he looked?

Probably.

Ben came into the house, a welcome interruption.

"Ben, there are clothes for you to change into in the bedroom to help us blend in," Derek told Ben.

"Ah, you are just in time for dinner. You can change after, Ben. Come sit here, Derek," Mary said, motioning to a chair. "Carter and Ben, we will pull up chairs for you from the living room."

"I'll do that for you," Derek said, glad for something to keep him busy. To keep him from making eye contact with Maria.

When he came back, everyone was seated around a steaming pot of chicken stew, warm bread, butter, and a few jars of homemade jam. He inhaled the delicious smells and sat down. Ben looked as though he wanted to inhale all the food in sight.

Everyone bowed their heads except Carter, Ben, and Derek, who looked at each other in confusion. Why was no one praying?

Maria looked up and caught Derek's eye, then motioned for him to bow his head, then did the same for Carter and Ben. A moment later, everyone looked up and started eating.

"This all looks delicious," Ben said, grinning.

Maria, who sat next to him, leaned closer to him and whispered, "I forgot to tell you that the Amish have silent prayer before meals."

Her scent tickled his nose, peaches and cherry blossoms mixed with something sweet. He couldn't help but enjoy it for a moment when it made him realize how close he was to her.

He nodded curtly and turned so it would fade away.

***

Nighttime in Unity was silent and serene. The only lights on were the dots of light in the sky and the orb that bathed the farms in creamy moonlight. Other than the occasional sound from a farm animal in the barn, nothing disturbed the sleeping residents of the community.

Even though it was Derek's turn to sleep, he couldn't. Instead, he sat by the window, looking for any signs of movement.

A scream sent panic whooshing into his system.

Maria!

He bolted out of bed and ran to her room, taking two steps at a time. He flung open the door after only a few seconds that it took for him to get there. Ben was right behind him.

Maria sat up in her bed, trembling, holding the blankets up to her chin in a death grip as if they would protect her. She looked around the room wildly.

Derek stood beside her. "What's wrong?"

"What happened?" Ben demanded, looking around the room.

The window was closed. Derek peered out onto the ground below for a prowler, but no one was in sight. The night was still.

"There was a man standing in my doorway." She took in gulps of air as if she had been holding her breath. "He was standing there, watching me, holding a gun. He ran away when I screamed."

Maybe he was still in the house.

109

"Stay here," Derek ordered Ben, then he raced down the steps, his long legs taking two at a time once more. He knew he was disturbing the quiet, but he didn't care. He checked every corner, every closet, all the doors and windows. No one was outside the house, and everything was locked and undisturbed. How had the intruder gotten in?

He returned to Maria's room, where Mary, Gideon and Carter surrounded her, concerned.

"Did the bad man come back?" Carter climbed up onto the bed and threw his arms around his mother. Maria rested her chin on his head, rubbing his back, comforting him when she was the one who should be comforted.

"Every lock, door and window is untouched. I don't know how he got in, if he did," Derek told them. "Or how he did it so quickly. I mean, I was up here in less than ten seconds. Then I ran downstairs to look for him."

"I saw him standing there!" Maria cried, tears flowing onto her cheeks as she pointed at the door. She covered her mouth and looked at Carter, probably realizing she was scaring him.

"Maybe you were dreaming. You've been through a lot this week, and sometimes dreams can seem so real—" Gideon offered.

"No," Maria cut him off. "I'm telling you, he was standing there watching me." She paused, rubbing the side of her head and looking at the floor. "I mean, I think it was real. Now I'm not sure."

110

Carter's eyes watered and Maria hugged him closer. "It'll be okay, Carter." He nodded into her chest.

"Well, thank the Lord nothing happened," Mary said, running a hand over her daughter's long hair. Derek wondered what it felt like. Was it as silky and soft as it looked?

He had no business thinking about such things.

"Look, there's no point in keeping everyone awake when you have an early morning tomorrow. You all go to bed and I'll keep watch," Derek suggested.

"All right. Get us if you need anything," Gideon said, walking downstairs with Mary. Ben followed them.

"Can I stay here with you?" Carter asked Maria. "Please?"

"Okay. Just for tonight."

"I'll stay up and look out the windows for the rest of the night and stay near your door," Derek told her.

"Thank you. You believe me, don't you?" Her wide eyes shone with emotion in the moonlight. "It was wrong of me to come here. If he's here, I'm putting my family and community in danger. We should leave."

Gideon did have a point—she had been through so much. Maybe the trauma was seeping into her subconscious, playing out in her dreams. There was no way the intruder could have gone up to the second floor and out of the house that fast, could he?

111

"Look, Maria, sometimes dreams can seem very real. Believe me, I know. After my wife died, I thought I saw and heard her." Derek paused, realizing he had given her too much information. "Look, let's wait until morning to make any decisions. Ben and I will be right here, keeping a lookout. Call us if you need anything at all."

Maria frowned at him, but he walked out, closed the door and went downstairs.

"Do you think he was really here?" Ben asked Derek quietly in the hall. "Or do you think she imagined or dreamt it?"

"I'm not sure," Derek said slowly. "After what she's been through, it would be understandable if she did imagine or dream it. The brain deals with trauma in different ways. But she seemed so sure—"

"Sometimes illusions and dreams seem very real."

"You've got that right," Derek said. Every time he dreamed of his friend Danny, it seemed so real until he woke up and realized it had been a dream. "Either way, we need to take precautions. Stay here with the family while I take a look around."

Derek went outside with a flashlight to check the property. He searched the ground for footprints. Even in summer with no snow, he had been trained to find footprints. If they were there, he'd find them. The only ones he saw were Mary's small footprints near the garden and ones from Gideon's work boots leading to the barn.

He circled the house twice, and there were no fresh footprints, especially none of someone running. No footprints, no sign of a break-in, and no sign of an intruder.

Had Maria been dreaming after all, or was he missing something?

***

"After what happened last night, I think I should leave so I don't put anyone in danger," Maria told Mary and Gideon the next morning in the kitchen.

"Even if someone was in the house, we don't want you to leave. This could be a test, and we choose to trust the Lord with our lives," Gideon said.

"We just got you back. We don't want you to leave." Mary wrapped her arm around Maria's shoulder. "We are not afraid."

"Derek and Ben think I was dreaming. That I was seeing things," Maria muttered, brows furrowed and arms crossed.

"We aren't sure either way, ma'am," Ben said. "We are still taking precautions."

Derek explained, "Well, don't take it personally, but when people endure traumatic experiences, the brain can react in different ways. Sometimes dreams just seem very real, depending on how deep of a sleep you were in." Derek stepped closer to the three of them and sighed. "Look, I searched the ground for prints several times. I ran upstairs as soon as you screamed and looked outside right after.

There's no way someone could have gone upstairs and run outside without us seeing them. So unless this man flew into your bedroom window, we don't see how it is possible the shooter was in your room last night."

"They could be right. Maybe you were dreaming," Mary offered, rubbing her shoulder in a motherly way.

Maria sighed. "It seemed so real. But maybe you're right."

"Please stay, Maria. We want you here," Gideon insisted.

After breakfast, Derek and Ben rode with the rest of the family in their buggy to church. The jostling and narrow wheels made Derek miss the smooth ride of his car. He preferred his car's pine tree air freshener to the scent of horse manure.

The church was packed. "This is also our school house. The upstairs is the school and the sanctuary, and we eat lunch downstairs," Maria explained.

"I'm impressed," Derek admitted. "That's very resourceful."

"I went to school here until I finished in eighth grade."

"What about high school?"

"The Amish don't go to high school. We believe that more education beyond eighth grade is prideful. Many boys learn a trade right after the eighth grade instead, sometimes by apprenticing," Maria told him as they went into the sanctuary. "Many of the girls help at home with the chores and cooking, but some of them also learn how to do jobs too, like becoming a teacher, nanny, or midwife."

How archaic, Derek thought. How could going to high school be prideful? He didn't understand, but he kept his opinions to himself.

"The men sit on this side and the women sit on that side," she told him, motioning. "See you after." She turned to Carter. "You sit with Derek and Ben, all right?"

"Okay, Mommy," Carter said, and slipped his small hand into Derek's as Maria walked away. Derek flinched at first, surprised by the child's sign of trust and affection. Then, he wrapped his long fingers around Carter's. His heart ached, knowing once this thug—or thugs—were caught, he'd probably never see the boy again.

Several of the men introduced themselves. Derek had expected them to look at him and Ben strangely and be wary of them, since they were outsiders, but the men were friendly.

"What brings you to Unity?" one of the men asked.

"We are here to protect Maria Mast," Ben said.

"A man is trying to scare her into keeping secrets about her ex-boyfriend's criminal past, so we would appreciate if you prayed for her safety," Derek told them, meaning what he said about prayer. If God really was willing to help, they needed all the prayer they could get.

"Definitely. We will pray for the Mast family," they answered solemnly, and the service began.

Maria was invited up to the front of the church. Ben and Derek sat in the back on the men's side.

"I ask for forgiveness for my sins, and I ask that you accept me back into your community. I repent and want to live a holy life once again," Maria said before the congregation, making eye contact with several people, including him. She looked brave and sure of herself, unlike how she had looked the night before. Her back was straight and she held her chin up, smiling as the congregation stood before her, nodding in approval.

"Welcome back to the church," the bishop said warmly, and Maria was practically glowing with joy as she returned to her seat.

It warmed his heart to see her so happy. She deserved happiness and safety. The church welcomed her with open arms. Derek envied how she truly belonged somewhere. He wasn't sure if he ever would belong anywhere with a certain group of people, except at work.

During the sermon, Derek felt like he was going to fall asleep several times after keeping watch for a phantom intruder most of the night. Unless Maria really had seen someone in her room.

His mind wrestled back and forth. He trusted Maria, yet he wondered how much her hurtful past had impacted her judgment of reality.

After the service, the congregation went downstairs for lunch. All the women set out pies, casseroles and sandwiches. Derek and Ben kept to themselves for most of the lunch, except when a man would occasionally introduce himself. But Derek and Ben were not here to make friends. They were here to protect Maria, and they wouldn't be here long anyway. Though he had to admit, Derek liked the way everyone was so close here, and how everyone pitched in and helped each other. It reminded him of the church he went to in Georgia as a child, and a rare pang of homesickness hit him.

This reminded him of home…and of his parents. His parents would have loved it here.

Ben left to take a walk around the building, just to check things out. A man approached Derek after a moment.

"Hi, I'm Simon Hodges," a young man said, standing in front of him. "I'm Anna Hershberger's boyfriend. Nice to meet you."

"You too," Derek said, barely taking his eyes off Maria.

"Have you met Anna?"

"No, actually."

"She's the one in the purple dress over there by the desserts," Simon said, gesturing toward a petite, beautiful young blonde woman talking to Mary.

"You and that other man are Maria's bodyguards?"

"Yes."

"I heard she gave you Robert's clothing," Simon observed. Finally, Derek looked at him. "She really loved Robert."

"What happened to him? She mentioned he was killed in an accident?" An invisible fist clenched his heart at the thought of how much suffering Maria had endured over the years. What must it have been like for her to lose her new husband, then try to escape an abusive boyfriend?

"He was killed accidentally by a woman driving in a snowstorm. She confessed to the family, but they never pressed charges. In fact, they forgave her, and now they are good friends."

"What?" He stared at Simon in disbelief. "I mean, I knew the Amish don't offer information to police officers during investigations, but now they are friends with the woman who killed Robert?"

"Yes. We leave justice to the Lord. We do not report crimes because we forgive, forget, and move on. And now something good has come of it." Simon seemed sure of his beliefs as he stood tall with his chin up.

Wow. Derek had no idea if he could forgive someone for accidentally killing someone he loved and then become friends with them. That would take a very special person indeed.

He knew he'd never forgive the man who killed his wife.

Working in law enforcement, he valued justice greatly. How had Maria felt about seeing her husband's killer go unpunished? Was that why she had rebelled and left the community?

It really was none of his business. He turned his eyes back to Maria, watching as Carter ran up to her, telling her about something with excitement in his eyes. Derek hoped he would make good friends here as the boy ran upstairs to play with the other kids.

He wondered if Maria would meet someone here and get married to a nice Amish man. He felt his heart wilt a little at the thought, then silently berated himself. She could marry whoever she wanted.

***

"Maria!" Liz Kulp ran up to Maria and grabbed her hands, kissing her on the cheek. "I'm so glad you're back. We missed you so much while you were gone."

"Thanks," Maria said with a smile. "I missed you all too."

Anna joined them and hugged Maria tightly, holding on for several seconds. She and Liz had been true friends for many years up until Maria had left. "Everyone is glad that you're back. Carter will love it here."

"You brought bodyguards, I heard?" Liz asked, her eyes sliding over to where Derek stood. Her voice dropped to a whisper as she pulled Maria and Anna into a quiet corner. "Why do you need bodyguards?"

"Wow, news travels fast." Maria chuckled nervously. "It's just a precaution. Someone tried to scare me at my house. They are just here to keep an eye on Carter and me. It's nothing to worry about."

"They are both so handsome. I wouldn't mind having someone like that around," Liz whispered with a giggle.

"I second that!" Anna chimed in, making a face at Liz and tucking a blonde wisp of hair back under her *kapp*. "Especially Ben. That's his name, right?"

"Yes, that's his name." Maria couldn't help but smile at her friends' laughter.

"What? I know we aren't supposed to remark on another person's outward appearance, but I just can't help it," Liz said, and Anna waved her hand in front of her face to get her to stop staring at Derek, laughing. "That one over there—is he nice?"

"What does it matter? He'll be leaving after his assignment is over. They both will. But yes, he is very nice. He can be funny sometimes, too. He's not always so serious." Maria watched as Derek stood stiffly in a corner with his arms crossed, watching everyone's movements silently, looking as approachable as a cactus.

"Well, it looks like you're in capable hands. Whoever tried to scare you, I bet your bodyguard will find him," Liz said in a hopeful voice.

"I hope so."

***

After lunch, they packed up the food and went back to the Mast farm. Carter ran through the door, shouting something about wanting to play another game with Gideon.

"Mommy! Look, there's a letter for you!" Carter called from the kitchen, and dread wrapped around Derek like a wet blanket.

A letter was in the kitchen that hadn't been there before they left for church?

"Hold on, Carter. Don't touch it!" Derek called. Derek pulled out his phone and took a photo of the note. He put on a pair of gloves and picked it up.

Derek carefully flipped over the note, and Maria appeared beside him. The front of the paper said Maria's name in large, block letters. He unfolded the note, being careful to only touch the very edges so he wouldn't get more prints on it. The white rectangle opened to reveal uppercase block letters that disguised the writer's handwriting.

Maria,

Meet me alone and unarmed at the old, broken-down barn at the end of the lane or deal with the consequences. I will let you know when.

Maria's small, pale hand gripped Derek's forearm as she read the note beside him, shooting warmth up his arm and into his chest, which was quickly replaced by a chilling fear. Her scent surrounded him again, clean linen and something flowery, but this time he ignored it and focused on the current situation. He slid the note into a plastic bag to send to CPDU for processing.

Derek doubted they would be able to find any prints on it, but it was worth a shot. The stalker probably wore gloves again, if he was smart. Judging by the way he had slipped in and out of the house without a trace last night, he was.

If Maria hadn't been dreaming.

"How in the world did he find us?" Maria cried out, her hands flying to her mouth.

"I have no idea," Derek answered. Had the stalker sent someone else to follow Maria's car? Derek had stared at those rearview mirrors, making sure the entire way that no one had followed them. Had he missed someone following them?

He had checked Maria's car for tracking devices and he had found it. So the stalker couldn't have tracked them there.

Unless…

Derek grabbed her keys and ran out the door.

Maria followed him out into the woods where they were hiding her car, having to take twice as many steps to keep up with Derek's long strides.

Maria usually loved being in the woods, listening to the birds chirp and watching for the movements of small animals in the bushes or the occasional deer. Now she was hyper-aware of every detail of her surroundings. The sounds that were once comforting to her now grated her nerves. Afternoon sunlight filtered through the trees in spotty, slanted rays, but it only made her shiver.

"You said you already checked the car for tracking devices," Maria said. "And you found one. So what's wrong?"

"I think there might have been more than one. That first one might have been a decoy. And if it was, I fell for it."

She watched Derek in anticipation as he ran his hands all over the outside of the car and underneath it. Anticipation turned into anxiety as the moments wore on. He opened the car and searched the inside, including under the seats. He popped the trunk and looked in there as well.

After she began pacing and biting her nails, Derek finally spoke. "There's nothing here. I checked thoroughly at your house, too." He let out a sigh that sounded more like a growl. "Wait… Give me your phone."

Maria had been keeping it on her to be safe. She pulled it from her apron pocket and handed it to him. "Why? What's wrong?"

"Has Trevor ever taken your phone, even for a minute? Do you always have it on you?"

"He's never taken this one, no. I got this one after I left him. And I always keep it on me. Why?"

"I was thinking maybe he could have taken it and set up something to track your location for your stalker if they were working together on this." Derek scrolled through her phones apps and settings. "If they ever got a hold of your phone, even for a minute, they could have set up a way to track you. I can't believe I didn't think of this sooner. Wait. What about the night Trevor came to your house? Did you turn away from your phone, even for a few seconds?"

"I might have… I'm not sure. I had a lot on my mind. It's possible. I don't remember," Maria said.

"No!" Anger boiled inside him, and Derek clenched his fist, trying to gain control over his display of emotion. Someone had taken Maria's phone and changed the settings, secretly sharing her location to their phone without Maria even realizing it. "They've been tracking you through your phone."

"What? How?"

"Someone took your phone, changed the setting that shares your location, then they sent an invitation from your phone to their phone to share your location indefinitely. Then they accepted the invitation on their own phone."

"But wouldn't I have seen that or noticed something?"

"It's all done through an app, and they hid the app so it was operating in stealth mode the entire time. You probably would have never noticed it. And it's untraceable. I have no way of knowing who this person is. I've heard of this happening before, but this is the first time I've actually seen it done. But that's no excuse." Derek shouted in frustration and Maria jumped at the sudden noise. He wanted to throw the phone on the ground as hard as he could, but that wouldn't do any good. Instead, he changed the phone's settings back to normal and deleted the app.

"Are you okay?" Maria asked.

"I'm sorry. Yes, I'm just angry at myself for not thinking of this sooner." He pressed the phone back into her hand. "Give that to Ben and have him double check everything. Just in case I missed something again."

Maybe he should be taken off this case. It was getting too personal. He cared about Maria too much, and it was starting to affect the way he did his job. He should just call Branson when he got back to the farm and ask for a replacement.

Uneasiness washed over him at the thought of some other person working with Banks and being responsible for keeping Maria and Carter alive, knowing he would rather do it himself.

But right now, he didn't trust himself.

He looked up and realized Maria was still standing there, arms wrapped around herself, watching him awkwardly as though she didn't know what to say.

"Everyone makes mistakes," she offered.

"A mistake on my end could get someone killed," he blurted hotly, then instantly regretted it.

Fear rose up in her eyes. She looked so vulnerable and scared that his protective instincts almost made him pull her into his arms. His arms even twitched at the thought, his hands about to reach for her, but he reined in the desire.

He let out a sigh. "I've protected political figures in even more dangerous situations and did better than this. Maria, I'm going to have someone replace me to protect you. I'm not doing as well as I usually do in situations like these." *Because I have never had feelings for the person I'm protecting before,* he finished silently.

Her dark eyes searched his, and for a moment he wondered if she'd read his mind. Then she took a step back and said, "I don't want anyone else to protect Carter and me but you and Ben."

"Of course Banks will stay, but whoever replaces me will do a better job. It's not fair to you that..." his sentence trailed off when he couldn't find the right words. "It's just better if you have a different bodyguard, someone other than me." With finality in his tone, he stomped off and Maria fell in step beside him.

Maria didn't argue as they walked back to the farm, but when he glanced over at her, her brow was furrowed and he couldn't quite read her expression. But if he had one guess, it would be disappointment.

As soon as Derek reached his room, he whipped out his cell phone and dialed Captain Branson's number.

"Branson here."

"It's Turner."

"You've got an update for me?"

"The perpetrator knows where we are. They hacked her phone and used an app to track her location. He left a note for her telling her to meet him alone or else she will have to pay the consequences."

"You didn't check her phone? That was a rookie mistake, Turner. Why didn't you?" The disappointment in his voice was clear.

"I was totally off my game. I didn't even think of it. I was distracted." Derek used his thumb and forefinger to rub his eyelids, the effect of voicing his mistake aloud weighing on him.

"By what? A tornado? A crashing space ship? It must have been something that really demanded your attention. You're better than this, Turner."

"I know. That's why I think you should have someone replace me."

"Can't. No one else is available. That's why I sent you Banks, the rookie, because I have no one else to spare who can help you protect this lady. I have the other officers and agents working on busting the trafficking ring and arresting the other pimps from the video footage. Everyone else is working on that string of burglaries downtown or training our new agents. The only other person who could replace you would be another rookie, if I can even find one that I can spare. We don't want that."

"No, no," Derek said quickly. He let out the breath he didn't realize he was holding. "So I'm stuck here?"

"Unfortunately, yes. I know you can do this, Derek. Just step up your game. You've had assignments much harder than this, Turner."

Actually, this one was the hardest. But he didn't want another rookie taking care of her, so he was going to have to reel in his emotions and get his head in the game.

"No problem, Branson. I've got it under control."

He hoped it was true. Because Maria's life depended on it.

CHAPTER NINE

Maria was eavesdropping. She knew it was wrong, but she didn't understand why Derek wanted a replacement. He made a small mistake anyone could have made. Why was he beating himself up over it so badly? Why was he ready to quit?

Was it because he felt something for her, or had she read him wrong? The way he looked at her, the connection she felt between them, the sparks she had felt when she had touched his arm…

"I'm stuck here?"

At the sound of his begrudging tone, her heart fell. She had been wrong. It was completely silly to think such a good looking, intelligent, and well-trained agent would like a person like her: a formerly abused woman with a kid, no job, no money, no education, going nowhere.

So why did he want to leave so badly?

She heard his phone beep off and she scrambled up the stairs quietly to her room. Searching for something to make herself look busy, she grabbed her sketchbook and sat at her desk with a pencil, flipping open the pages of drawings. She had her row of drawing pencils set out on her desk, all perfectly aligned. Maria wasn't very particular about many things, but ever since she was little, she always was obsessive about keeping her pencils sharp for school and artwork. She hated using a pencil that wasn't sharp enough.

A knock sounded on her door.

"Come in." Her heart thudded. Had he seen her running up the steps? Did he know she had been listening?

His tall, muscular frame filled the doorway as he stepped inside. "I'm sorry for how I acted in the woods. I lost it."

"It's okay," she said, turning in her chair to face him.

"There is no replacement available, so I'll be staying."

She searched his face for any hint of emotion, but she saw none. Had she really been completely wrong about him? Or was he an unfeeling person who only cared about professionalism?

"What's that?" he asked, nodding toward her sketchbook.

She slammed it shut in a panic at his question, her heart racing. She hadn't meant for him to look at it. Folded somewhere within those pages was a drawing of his face that she had been working on the past few days.

"Just some drawings. I like to draw. Robert taught me how. It was one thing I could do that my ex couldn't control because he didn't know about it. I kept it hidden."

"Can I see your drawings?"

Maria saw mischief light up in Derek's eyes. She knew what was coming. He darted for the spiral-bound book. She snatched it away from his reach, leaping out of her chair. He lunged again, grinning.

130

Maria couldn't help but let out a laugh at their game, at the rare revealing of his silly side that was a refreshing change from his usual serious self. But dread crept into her chest again, sweeping over her as he outsmarted her, swiping away the book with a haughty laugh of victory.

"It's nothing interesting," she stammered, hoping he'd have a quick look and hand it back. "I just do it for fun."

The grin fell from his face and was replaced with an impressed expression. He silently took in every picture, studying each one, slowly turning the pages. Horses pranced across some pages, and some were of people she saw on the street or images she made up in her mind, like landscapes and architecture of faraway, European places.

"Maria, these are incredible!" he exclaimed, looking up at her.

Heat burned her cheeks in embarrassment at his compliment.

"I'm serious. You're amazing," he said.

She smiled, reluctantly accepting his praise.

"At drawing," he added, looking back at the pages.

What else would he mean?

The realization that he was about to turn to the drawing of him sent her heart into panic mode. She grabbed it out of his hands without thinking and hugged it to her chest. "The rest is private, thank you very much."

"Can I just—" He reached for it.

"No," she said a little more firmly than necessary. His seriousness returned, his demeanor changing as if someone had dumped a bucket of ice water on his head.

"I'm sorry. It's none of my business," he mumbled, adjusting his glasses awkwardly, then he backed out of the room.

She let out a breath of relief, then guilt nudged its way in. She hadn't meant to snap at him. But he had been right. Her personal life and interests were none of his business.

***

That night, Maria couldn't sleep. She kept seeing the angry words of the note in her mind. She kept remembering the figure lurking in her doorway from the other night. She knew she hadn't been dreaming. The memory burned within her mind, an image she couldn't erase.

Frustrated after hours of no sleep, she walked quietly down the steps, careful to avoid the creaky spots. She didn't want to wake anyone up. She just wanted a quick glass of water. Then she would turn on a battery-operated light and read until she was sleepy.

She tip-toed past the spare room and her parents' room. The night was so still and warm, and with no air conditioning. The humidity was thick and sticky on her skin. An orchestra of crickets and bullfrogs played outside, calming her frayed nerves.

"Can't sleep?" Ben asked, standing in the kitchen. Ben and Derek took turns staying up and sleeping so that one of them was always on guard.

"No... I have too much on my mind." She got a glass out of the kitchen cabinet and filled it with sink water, then gulped down the cool liquid.

Maria turned to take it back up to her room when suddenly the feeling of being watched sank into her bones. She froze and looked around the house, half expecting an intruder to leap out behind the curtains or a shadowed corner.

"What?" Ben asked.

"I felt like... Nothing." Ben was standing right there. She was being paranoid. No one was watching her. She continued walking to the stairs, taking a calming breath.

Something caught her eye. She saw the silhouette of a man outside walking slowly by the outside window. The outline of a face appeared in between the curtains, peering at her eerily.

The glass of water fell from her hands as they rose to her mouth to stifle a scream. Shards scattered across the floor with a loud crash.

"Derek!" The word erupted from her mouth in a panic. Ben was already bolting out the door and into the night to chase after the stalker.

She stood as though glued to the floor as Derek scrambled from the spare room into the kitchen, gun ready and fully awake. Before he could say anything, she pointed to the window, her heart pounding in her ears. "Someone was looking in the window! Ben went after him."

"Go lock yourself in a bedroom," Derek ordered.

Her parents and son ran into the kitchen.

"What's wrong?" Gideon demanded, Mary trailing behind him, then Carter emerged from his room.

"Get in a bedroom now! Go!" Derek commanded. They all scrambled into the nearest bedroom and shut the door behind them.

"Stay away from the windows," Derek said from the hall.

"Someone was watching me through the window," she explained to her family.

Wrought with worry, she sent a prayer heavenward. She turned and faced her family. It was not fair to the people of Unity that she endanger their lives by living among them.

"That's it. I can't have this man snooping around, trying to break into your house to get to me. We're leaving tonight. This ends now," Maria announced, finality in her voice.

All three of them objected at once, but she put her hand up. "There's no point in arguing with me. I can't put you all in danger any longer. Derek, Ben, Carter and I will leave so you can all be safe again. And then when we are safe again, we will come back."

"Maria, you know we trust God with our safety. Derek and Ben are here to protect us," Mary persisted, following her up to her room.

"*Maam,* this is my decision. There's no changing my mind. If something happened to any of you because of me, I just couldn't live with myself." The words caught in her throat, clenching her chest at the thought of one of her family or friends dying at the hands of the stalker.

She'd suffered enough. She couldn't bear losing someone else.

Defeated, her mother asked, "You think Ben's all right?"

"He's a trained field agent and bodyguard. He'll be fine," she said, pushing aside the uneasiness and worry for his safety that swelled up inside her.

A few moments later, Derek said, "Ben is back. You can come out now." He opened the door and they all stepped out.

Ben tried to catch his breath. "He's fast. I couldn't catch up to him. He's gone. Did you get a good look at his face, Maria?" he asked, bending over to rest his hands on his knees.

"No, I only saw the outline of his face. It was so dark," Maria said. "I'm sorry."

He waved away her apology. "It's not your fault. You know, I think there were two or three of them. I heard some rustling coming from the trees and saw some movement. It could have been an animal, but there could have been a second or third perp."

"We're definitely leaving. Tonight. I don't want to endanger this town any longer," Maria said.

"If that's what you want, then we can do that," Derek said. "Mary and Gideon, you should come with us. You shouldn't stay here unprotected."

"No. This is our home. We will stay here. God will protect us," Gideon answered, and Mary nodded.

"Then at least let me ask CPDU if they can spare someone to protect you. Even to drive by and check on you every now and then," Derek offered, pulling his phone out of his pocket.

"No, no. No police. As Gideon said, the Lord will protect us." Mary shook her head.

Derek held back an argument. How could they refuse protection in a situation like this? "Please, let me at least have an officer check on you."

"Didn't you see what just happened? What if they come after you?" Maria cried.

"No. Please. We don't want it. We appreciate the offer though," Gideon said. "Maria, you haven't officially rejoined the church yet so you can have police protection if you want. We will only trust the Lord to protect us."

"You won't be able to change their minds," Maria whispered to Derek.

"Fine. But at least please call me if anything changes," Derek said, sighing in defeat.

As they drove the car into the driveway and packed it up, Maria and Carter said goodbye to Gideon and Mary. By now, the sun was beginning to rise.

"This is only temporary. I'll come back once this stalker is caught," Maria promised.

Carter hugged his grandparents. "I want to stay. I'll miss all the animals."

"You'll be back soon," Mary assured him. "We just got you back. We hate to see you leave."

Gideon wrapped Maria in a warm hug. "Come back soon, you hear? We love having you back. We will be praying for your safe return."

"Yes," Mary said, taking Maria into her arms once Gideon let her go. She wiped a tear from her eye. "We will be praying. Derek. Please keep her safe so she can come home soon."

"Yes, ma'am. We better go, Maria," Derek said solemnly, packing the last of the bags into the car.

Maria and Carter said their final goodbyes, and they drove away. Carter stared out the window behind them, watching Mary and Gideon waving as they stood in the driveway. The farm shrank more and more as the sun began to rise higher, painting the sky with orange, golden and pink hues.

***

Not even an hour had passed when Derek's cell phone rang. Ben drove ahead of them again in his car.

"It's your parents," he said. They had given them Derek's phone number earlier. He swiped the screen as Maria drove and he turned it on. "Hello?"

"Derek? Something has happened," Gideon's voice trembled over the phone. "In the barn."

"What is it?"

"I went out to the barn to feed the animals, and the stalker killed one of our lambs, leaving a note that said he would do the same to a family member if Maria left the Amish community. What do you think? Should you bring her back here? Or is it better if she stays away?"

Derek let out a long whoosh of air, indecision bouncing around in his brain. If he brought her back there, the stalker would know her whereabouts. If he didn't, someone could get killed, and he knew Maria would rather risk her own safety than risk someone else's.

It was a no-win situation.

"What? What's happened?" Maria demanded from the driver's seat.

He had no choice but to tell her, and when he did, color drained from her face. "We have to go back," she said.

"Are you sure?"

"This guy isn't bluffing. I have no doubt he could kill someone just to get to me. We have to do what he says. I couldn't stand to lose anyone else," she added in a quiet voice.

Derek called Ben, then they decided to return. Maria whipped the car around and drove back the way she had come.

After they pulled up the farm driveway, Carter teared up. "That poor lamb. I'm sad it's dead. That man is very mean."

"Yes, Carter. I'm sorry. When we get there. maybe you can play a game with your grandparents. Won't that be fun?" Maria asked. "Then you'll forget all about it."

"I won't forget. It makes me sad that the lamb is dead."

The image of Natalia's dead body on his apartment carpet and the memory of her blood soaking the floor flashed through Derek's mind. No, he would never forget that for as long as he would live.

Carter and Ben went with Mary and Gideon inside the house.

Derek and Maria entered the barn, where flies were already gathering. Derek took hold of Maria's arm protectively.

"Maybe you shouldn't see this."

She pulled away from his grip.

"I'm fine. I'm sure I've seen worse," she muttered, and he didn't doubt her as she approached the area of the barn where the lambs were kept.

Still, her hands flew to her mouth to muffle a gasp when she saw the small animal's sliced throat, the innocent body left mangled on the hay. She turned away, now facing him, and Derek instinctively opened his arms where she melted into his comforting hug. Her warm, soft frame fit perfectly under his chin, and once again her scent teased his senses. He would have been glad to have her stay there, but it only lasted for a moment. Suddenly she seemed to realize what she was doing and she wiped her tears and put distance between them.

"Sorry. It's just that lambs are so innocent. This animal didn't deserve this," she said with a sniff, regaining her composure.

Tenderness filled him at her love for animals. He didn't share the same compassion; he was just thankful it hadn't been a human. The lamb had taken the fall, and briefly he was reminded of the Lamb of God who took the punishment of the world to save those who believe in Him from eternal damnation.

But this was completely different. This lamb had died at the hands of a crazed thug who was trying to show his power.

Derek reached for a piece of paper that had been left near the lamb. He unfolded the note and read aloud.

Maria, I watched you pack up your car with your son and bodyguard, then saw you drive away. You think you can escape that easily? If you leave the community or move out of your house, I will kill one of your friends or family members like I killed this lamb. Meet me at the barn alone or deal with the consequences. I will let you know when to meet.

A chill swept over him as he read the words, and it apparently had the same effect on Maria. She wrapped her arms around herself as he wished he could pull her into his arms again to comfort her.

"So we have to stay here, I guess," Derek mumbled.

Maria nodded, staring at the note. "I should meet him. Then no one else will get hurt."

"No. No way," he snapped, then took on a more gentle tone. "My job is to protect you. I can't let you do that."

"So you expect me to just watch idly while people I love die around me? We have to end this!"

"We will. I'm going to catch him. He's smart, but eventually everyone makes mistakes, and when he makes his, I'll be ready with handcuffs." Determination rang through his voice.

He saw stubbornness flicker in her eyes before she spun on her heel and walked back into the house.

She better not be getting any heroic, reckless ideas.

CHAPTER TEN

After Ben and Derek checked every room in the house, Maria set her bags on her bed, sighing in defeat. She was back on the farm, endangering the lives of everyone in the community. There was no way out, as if she was lost deep in the forest with no compass.

She began to unpack, then noticed a paper on her pillow, tucked under her quilt so only the corner was peeking out. Another note? In her bedroom, of all places? Disgust trickled over her and her stomach churned as she opened the folded paper with shaking hands.

All it said was, *Tonight at midnight.*

It was the time to meet the stalker in the barn. He had crept into her room and left it there, probably figuring that Derek and Ben wouldn't see it there if she didn't show them. And she couldn't show them. They'd only stop her.

This was the right thing to do. At midnight she would give herself up to the stalker. For the sake of everyone she loved, she had to do it.

***

That night, Maria stealthily slipped on a pair of boots, trying to calm her nerves. Anxiety and dread sat like a rock in her stomach as she tied her sheets together to make a makeshift rope, just like she'd seen in movies. She only had to get to the top of the porch, then she could climb down the rest of the way. There was no way she'd be able to sneak down the stairs and past Ben or Derek, whoever was keeping watch, and out the door.

Am I making the right choice? Maria wondered for the hundredth time. She pictured the faces of her friends and family, imagining the grief, despair, and regret she'd feel if anything happened to them because of her.

I couldn't live with that, she thought.

This was the right choice.

She loved her family and friends too much to see them die at the hands of whoever was stalking her. There was no way she'd be able to live with herself after that.

In fact, she'd rather die.

Maria gripped the flashlight in her hand with white knuckles and shoved it into her backpack, praying no one would hear her creep out into the night.

Maria tied the sheet rope to her bed and flung it out the window, then shimmied down slowly. They made it look so much easier in the movies. She finally got low enough to drop down onto the top of the porch. She flinched, hoping Ben or Derek wouldn't hear the thud. She waited, but no one came outside, so she breathed a sigh of relief and climbed down onto the porch, then crept down the porch stairs and into the yard.

As she stepped outside into the darkness, she knew that not surviving tonight was a very real possibility. Fear gnawed at her mind, but she kept moving through the night. The wet grass licked her boots as she walked on, staring at the old crooked barn looming in the distance. Several boards had fallen off its frame years ago, and the roof sagged in the middle. The moonlight outlined it in a silvery glow, only adding to its eeriness. She wasn't far now.

When Maria arrived, she stood outside the structure and stared at it, doubts assailing her again. Was she really doing the right thing? Would offering herself as a sacrifice really protect her community?

Would he torture her, trying to get information she knew nothing about? And would he kill her when she was done talking? She didn't know, but she would do whatever it took to protect her family and friends.

Maria walked forward and took hold of the door, slowly opening as it creaked in protest. The inside of the barn looked as dilapidated as the outside did, as though ghosts resided there during the night. She was about to open her mouth and call out for the stalker when the barn door flew open.

She spun around and saw the outline of a man in the moonlight, and fear flowed through her veins like an injected poison. Now it was too late to change her mind. Her fate had been sealed.

Would she die here?

"Maria!" the man called out, his deep voice soothing her frazzled nerves like a rich ointment.

Relief washed over her when she realized it was Derek, who then covered the distance between them in only a few long strides and grasped her shoulders.

He was going to be so infuriated with her.

He whispered, "What were you thinking, coming out here? Let's go right now before he comes and—"

Derek froze when a shuffling noise sounded from the corner of the barn. Maria's heart rate doubled as she saw a shadow slide across the barn wall. Derek gripped his 9mm tighter.

The stalker was already here. He must have seen her leave the house, constantly watching her. Maria's stomach clenched, then a sickening feeling filled her.

"Couldn't stay away, could you?" he seethed from an unknown place in the barn concealed by shadows.

Derek stood in front of her. She could feel the bravery and strength radiating from his body. If he was afraid, he didn't show it.

"She doesn't know any information about the trafficking ring. She didn't tell anyone anything!" Derek shouted.

"Walk away, mister. Leave her with me, and no one gets hurt," came the command from the darkness.

"No. I can't do that," Derek said sternly.

"I just want to ask her some questions."

"We both know there will be more to it than that." He turned to Maria and whispered fiercely, "Run!"

They bolted for the door, and gunfire shattered the stillness of the night as the stalker fired warning shots. Clearly he didn't want Maria dead, and since she was so close to Derek, the shooter wouldn't risk hitting her, so he was firing at nothing. But if he was trying to scare her, it was working. Her heart pounded in her ears as they raced toward the woods. Derek had a strong grip on Maria's hand as he led her to safety, and if she hadn't been so terrified, she would have enjoyed the feeling of his warm hand in hers. They wove in and out of trees, trying to zigzag their way to safety.

"I think we lost him," Derek panted as they slowed to a stop in the woods.

Maria knew the woods well and knew exactly where they were. Moonlight sifted through the trees, lighting Derek's angry face in silvery splotches. He led her back to the farm in silence, dropping her hand.

She braced herself for his lecture.

"I told you not to meet him. What were you thinking?" The words sputtered out of his mouth like hot sparks from a fire, and she jumped back as though she had been burned.

"I didn't want anyone to be hurt on my account," she shot back. "Did you really think I'd be fine risking everyone else's safety and doing nothing about it?"

Derek looked like he wanted to pull his hair out. He paced sporadically across the kitchen. "I can't do my job if you won't cooperate. You have to do what I say. You can't just go meet your death in the middle of the night."

"But I thought that he needs me alive to see what I know."

"Don't you realize what that means? He probably intends to torture you, find out what you know, and then kill you when he's finished. Who knows? You think he'd let you see him and then live to tell about it?"

"Of course I thought about that. But I'd do anything to save my family. Besides, I was kind of hoping you would figure it out and rescue me before it came to that."

He let out a long breath. "Of course I would try to rescue you. I'd do anything to keep you safe. I wouldn't rest until I found you," he said, his voice gentle now. He lifted a hand and before she knew what was happening, his finger was tracing the outline of her jaw. She looked into his eyes, and his gaze dropped from her eyes to her lips. For a moment, she wondered if he was going to kiss her. Then he turned away.

Had he said that because it would be his job to find her, or did he really care about her like she cared for him?

"How did you know I had left?"

"I was keeping watch while Ben slept and I knew something wasn't right. When I checked on you and you weren't in your bed, I

147

knew right away that the stalker had given you a time and that you had gone to the barn. When I saw the rope you made out of sheets, that confirmed it. Ben stayed with your family and I ran out there as fast as I could. It looks like I got there just in time. You need to promise me that you won't ever do anything like that again. Okay? Do you promise?"

She sighed. "I promise."

***

The next morning, after finishing breakfast, Gideon went to work and Mary left to run errands and visit a friend. Derek and Ben stayed at the house with Maria so they could keep a close eye on her.

While Ben rested, Maria put all of the dishes in the kitchen sink. Derek sidled up to her and nudged her to the side.

"I'll wash. You can dry them and put them away," he said, filling the sink with soapy water.

"I told you that men don't do kitchen chores here." She pulled towels out of a drawer and wiped down the table.

"I'm not Amish so that rule doesn't apply to me. So just let me do it."

She turned enough so he could see her smiling.

"Thank you."

"No problem."

"Why did you leave here? Was it because of Freya and what happened to your husband? I heard she accidentally killed him." The questions slipped out before he thought about it twice.

He stared out the window at the perfect green hills. This Amish community seemed like its own little perfect world. Except now, with a crazed stalker on the loose.

"Yes, she did. She was on the run from her abusive ex-fiancé, and he had connections with the police. Freya was afraid he'd find her if the accident went on the record. She was so terrified that she left Robert there in the road. Just left him, there like forgotten rubbish. That was the hardest part for me to accept. I don't know how she could have done that." Maria rubbed a plate with her towel harder than necessary, her face reddening. "But then she felt so guilty that she tracked Robert's parents down and told them the truth. I was at their house that day."

"Simon told me you all forgave her, and now you're friends," Derek said.

"Yes, we did. It was hard, but we did. Robert was kind and loving, and it's what he would have wanted. We were going to buy a small piece of land and build a farmhouse with a barn. We planned on filling it with children. But Robert died before Carter was even born.

"After Robert died, I shut everyone out. I really loved him, and the grief hit me so hard I wasn't thinking straight, you know?" Maria said, putting a cup in the cabinet.

149

"Actually, I do," he murmured, dunking a plate into the soapy water.

Time had healed much of his sorrow, and sometimes he went most of the day without thinking of Natalia or remembering her death. But some days the memories brought a physical pain in his chest.

"So, did you leave because there was no justice for Robert's death?" Derek asked.

"Well, I was angry until I met Freya. Even after I forgave Freya, I just wasn't the same person anymore. There were a lot of reasons, but I realized I just didn't belong here anymore, so I left. Then I met Trevor. I had grieved a good amount but was still heartbroken. I was very vulnerable because I had just left home. He knew that and used it to his advantage."

Anger coursed through Derek at how Trevor had manipulated and conned the young and naïve Maria, who had probably been sheltered from evil most of her life. Of course she wouldn't recognize the red flags of a con artist. He knew he would never know the amount of pain Trevor had caused her.

He wished he could get his hands on that guy and punch him for every time he had ever hurt Maria, verbally or physically. But of course that would never happen. It wouldn't solve their problems, and it wouldn't take back what Trevor had put her through.

"After a while, he tried to convince me to move in with him, but I stuck to my Amish ways in that area and never gave in. That's when the abuse started. He was trying to coerce me into living with him, but instead it pushed me away. I left him, moved away, changed my hair and got a job under a fake name. That was two years ago. For a while, it worked out. Then he found me, and that's when I went to CPDU."

"Why didn't you just come back here and live with your family?" Derek asked.

"Believe me, I wanted to come back, but I was too afraid he'd find me and hurt them."

Derek winced at the thought. No, that wouldn't have been good.

He gave a sideways glance at Maria, admiring her bravery, resourcefulness and love for her family. She really was willing to do anything for them.

Even give up her life for them.

"But I have put them in danger anyway, and now he won't let me leave." She sighed. "Okay, enough about my miserable past. What about you? Your family?" She put a stack of dried clean plates in the cabinet.

"I'm an only child. My parents were killed almost ten years ago. A burglar invaded their house. The burglar shot them both when my dad pulled out his gun. I'm not close to my other relatives because they live in other states, so I don't really have any family," Derek said, memories shuddering through his mind, especially when he had found the bodies. He really didn't want to think about it. "That's why I left the Marines. I joined CPDU and became a police officer, then a bodyguard. The killer was eventually caught after robbing several other homes, but I wanted to make sure every family got justice for crimes committed against loved ones."

Derek didn't know why he was opening up to her so much, but she was listening so intently, leaning up against the sink, so his words continued to spill out. He pulled out a chair and sat down.

Maria followed suit, resting her elbows on the table and watching him.

"In the Marines, I did one tour in Afghanistan, and one in Iraq. I lost a lot of friends. There's one memory that still haunts me, even though it was several years ago. I still have nightmares about it. I was with my friend Danny, guarding weapons. I left his side for a moment to get some water. While I was shielded by a building, he was shot and killed right in front of me. I didn't react quick enough to save him." Guilt spread through him like a toxic chemical, and he looked up in surprise when he felt Maria's hand covering his own.

"There's probably nothing you could have done," she offered.

"I might have been able to warn him if I had been paying attention. Or shielded him or knocked him out of the way." The memory of Danny's body on the sandy ground washed over him, the color of the blood on the dirt...

"We all make mistakes. Believe me, I know. I've made colossal ones. But God forgives us and gives us more chances," she said softly.

He leaned back in his chair, pulling his hand back, even though he wished he could let her keep holding his hand like that. It shot tenderness straight through his heart, and for a moment he remembered what it felt like to be loved by one woman. He wanted that kind of love again more than anything.

"I'm not the Christian I used to be. But I want to be close to God again. I envy the faith of your community. I haven't been able to bring myself to pray ever since..." He closed his eyes as images of Natalia's dead body assaulted him.

"Ever since your wife was killed?"

He opened his eyes to see Maria's understanding expression.

She said, "I'll admit it was hard for me to speak to God, too, after Robert was killed. Right when I quit on my own relationship with God, that's when I made all those horrible choices. I lost everything because of those choices. Now I know I need God, and I need to speak with him and read His Word, or else I'm just a mess. I can't rely on myself. I need Him to guide me."

He knew she was right. "It's not that I'm mad at God. I understand He gave us free will and doesn't control us, that we live in a fallen world. Sin was not a part of His plan. I don't know why, but I just don't pray anymore or read the Bible like I used to. I wish I did."

Maria sighed. "You seem afraid to open yourself up to His love. He won't leave you, Derek. He'll always be there for you. You just need to start. It'll get easier."

He looked into her expressive eyes as her words shot straight to his heart. "You're very perceptive, and absolutely right," he whispered. "That's exactly what it is. I'm so used to the ones I love dying that I'm afraid to love anyone else again. I hope one day I can get close to God again."

"Just ask Him for help. You can do it."

Maria's encouragement warmed his soul. She was right, and he now vowed to work on his relationship with God. She had made him see things differently. If he wasn't Maria's bodyguard, would he let himself fall in love with her? Or would he let fear of losing her hold him back?

He would never know.

"I'm going to hate to leave here. Everyone is so close. I've never known such a tight-knit place," he said. "I am growing to love the slower pace of life and the simplicity of it all. Out there, everything is so loud and chaotic. Everyone is always on social media, not deeply communicating. Here, people take the time to get to know each other and help each other. There really is a sense of community here."

"That's what we're known for," Maria said, then paused. "So, would you ever get married again if you met the right person?" she asked, her expression now unreadable.

Well, that certainly was a random question, but Maria was full of surprises. "I don't know. My job takes over my life, and I like it that way. Keeps me busy. But it's really dangerous. Not only for me, but for anyone close to me. I make many enemies, enemies that don't hesitate before killing people I love. Like the thug who killed my wife. He did it just to get back at me for arresting his brother. Now that I don't have a family, I'm not putting anyone I love in danger with my job."

Something flashed across Maria's face for only a fleeting moment. Disappointment? Pity? It was too quick for him to figure it out. But he was leaning more toward disappointment.

CHAPTER ELEVEN

After dinner, Maria leaned back from the table, feeling tired from a long, hot day of work. She had done all the laundry, which had taken up most of the day. She had used their old-fashioned Maytag washer which was run by gas. It swished the clothes back and forth, and then she put the wet garments through a wringer that squeezed most of the water out. She rinsed the dresses, undergarments, pants and shirts in a bucket and sent them through the wringer again. Then she hung the laundry out on the clothesline.

Maria had forgotten how long doing laundry took without electricity, but it was just another thing she would have to get used to again.

She had also scrubbed the floors, made lunch and dinner, and had done all the dishes by hand, just to name a few chores. That was one thing about being Amish that she didn't love. The dishes were never ending, and they had to be done by hand three times a day. She was really beginning to miss her dishwasher.

Derek and Ben had helped her with all of the chores, since they had to be with her all day anyway. Occasionally, one of them would nap, since they were each only sleeping half of each night, taking turns keeping watch.

Carter followed them around and also helped with what he could, like folding laundry or sweeping the floor, if you could call it sweeping. It was more like pushing dirt around with the broom. But Maria wanted him to feel like he was helping.

"That was a delicious meal, Maria. I forgot how great of a cook you are. We really missed your cooking while you were gone," Gideon said, rubbing his belly.

"She is a wonderful cook. Have you tried her bacon alfredo?" Derek piped in.

"That sounds delicious," Ben said.

"I hope you missed me for more than my cooking, *Daed*!" Maria laughed.

"Of course we did. We missed *you*. It's so good to have you back." Gideon smiled warmly at her.

"I appreciate all your help today. It gave me more time to spend visiting Mrs. Johnson. Why don't I do all the cleaning up and you go enjoy the rest of the evening?" Mary offered, getting up from the table and gathering plates.

"Thank you. I have to admit, it will take me some time to get back into the swing of things. I'm exhausted." Maria rubbed her lower back. "I'd like to take a walk." She needed some air, even if it was hot outside, and to stretch out her tired legs.

"Sounds good," Derek said, rising to join her. "Ben, you stay here."

Carter pulled out the deck of cards to play with Gideon. Their laughter floated out onto the porch as Maria and Derek walked down the porch steps.

The sun sat low in the sky, casting a warm glow over the fields. Derek's long legs carried him quickly and effortlessly, and Maria felt as though she had to jog to keep up.

"So, is all that work really worth it? You are rejoining the Amish even though you have to do all your chores by hand and they take twice as long as they should?" Derek asked.

"Of course it's worth it. It just takes some getting used to."

"I don't think I could do my laundry with that old Maytag washer like that for the rest of my life." Derek chuckled. "It is so much easier to throw it in the washing machine and dryer at home. Though I have to admit, there is something captivating about this place. People take time to visit each other instead of texting. You play board games together instead of watching TV. You pray at every meal. You all truly know each other. Your family seems so perfect." Envy crept up in his voice, and Maria guessed he was missing his own parents. "I will probably never have a family again. You should be very thankful."

"I am. I'm so glad to have them back. Who knows? Maybe you will have a family one day. People change their minds." Hope filled her for only a moment before she squashed it. He had made it perfectly clear that he didn't intend to ever marry. She steered her mind in another direction. "You know, our life wasn't always so 'perfect'." She made quotation marks with her hands.

"Really? Do tell." He smirked at her jokingly.

"Really. There was once a killer on the loose here targeting the Amish. Olivia and her husband Isaac solved the case and the killer was arrested, though they weren't married back then. The killer did horrible things to this community. We lived in fear. However, Robert was alive back then. I wish Carter could have met his father." Memories of his smile filled her mind, though each time she thought of his face, she remembered less and less. She had no photographs of him because the Amish were against being in pictures.

"You know, you've done a fine job raising Carter on your own. I don't know how single moms do it," he said with admiration.

"Do you want kids someday?" she blurted. It was such a common question that she hadn't thought twice. But she shouldn't be asking *him* such a thing.

"If I didn't work at CPDU, then I definitely would. I work all the time. Plus, I couldn't put them in danger because of my job. If someone wanted to get back at me, they could take it out on my kids. I couldn't live with that. But if my parents were alive, I am sure they would have loved to be grandparents. They'd be begging me for grandkids." He smiled as his own memories seemed to surface.

"Your parents sound like people I'd like to have met."

"You would have liked them. My mom would have swapped recipes with you. My dad would have shown you his record collection."

They walked on in silence, then Derek stopped. "We should get back."

"It was nice to get out of the house. I was feeling a little claustrophobic."

"Do we have to do housework again tomorrow?" Derek asked, making a face.

"Of course. The dishes will get dirty again, and we will have to cook more food."

"I'm so glad I'm not Amish. I really couldn't do laundry and dishes all the time," Derek said, walking back to the house.

"You're a man. You wouldn't have to do those things. If you did what my father does, you'd wake up early to feed the animals, work at the cabinet shop, keep the firewood supply stocked, and other things like that. No kitchen chores for you."

"Oh, good. That would be a real deal breaker. I might be good at dishes, but I sure wouldn't want to do a pile of them by hand every day."

Maria glanced at him to see his grin. She looked away before he could catch her eye. He didn't have to worry about such things, even though she knew he was joking. He would never become Amish. They were from two completely different worlds.

After returning to the house, they played a game of Dutch Blitz before getting ready for bed. Derek laughed, and they even got a few chuckles out of Ben while the two bodyguards kept watch as the family played.

Maria laughed harder than she had in a long time. It felt so good to laugh freely with her family without having to worry about anyone criticizing the sound of her laugh.

Just as Maria was starting to relax, she remembered the threat against her and her family. Was it wrong of her to be having such a good time when there was a predator after her?

She knew she shouldn't live her life in fear, so she let herself pretend there was no stalker, just for a little while.

***

"Are you sure you will be okay without us?" Mary asked the next day and stopped packing her bag. "I can stay here if you would like."

"No. We will be fine. You should go. I never met *Daed's* Aunt Merle, but you knew her. She will want to see you." Besides, if the stalker came while they were gone, she was not in any more danger without them here.

"I'm sorry we have to go like this, but she could pass away any day. Gideon would be very heartbroken if he did not get to say goodbye." Mary zipped up her bag and carried it out to the door, where Gideon was putting on his shoes.

161

"We will be back in a few days. Make sure all the animals are fed. Hopefully, the cabinet shop will be fine without me," Gideon said with a smile. "I am not worried about leaving the farm in your capable hands. And Sid Hoffman and Mrs. Johnson were so gracious to offer their help with the chores." His expression grew serious. "And we will pray for your safety while we are gone."

"Don't worry. I will take good care of the animals!" Carter piped in, looking confident in himself. "Mom will help me."

"Oh, good. Well, I definitely won't worry about the animals then." Gideon chuckled.

"Thank you. We'll be fine. Don't worry about us." She didn't mean for the admiration to surface in her voice, but it did anyway. "Have a good trip."

After hugs and goodbyes, Maria watched her parents drive away in their buggy. She had to admit, it would be nice to have the house to themselves for a few days.

She turned to face Derek, who had been standing out of the way in the kitchen, and sighed. "I wish we could drive to the beach or do something fun out of town. It would be fun for Carter to do something other than hang around the farm all the time, even though he doesn't seem to mind it."

"I know," he said, walking toward her slowly. "But I'm afraid if we leave, the criminal will think we are leaving town for good and will do something about it."

Derek glanced at Carter, who seemed oblivious to their conversation as he played with a puzzle on the sunny living room floor. But Maria knew he was listening.

"Well, what if we just do something outside, then? Like a picnic in the yard?" she suggested.

"A picnic?" Carter's head shot up. "Yeah!"

Derek frowned. "We'd be right out in the open for an extended amount of time. I don't think that's such a good idea anymore, not after what happened."

"What about an indoor picnic?" Ben suggested.

"Yeah! We could pretend we are outdoors. In the jungle!" Carter stood up, excitement showing on his face. "I'm going to decorate the whole living room." He got right to work, pulling paper and his crayons out and spreading them onto the floor.

"Okay, then. As long as I don't have to make the food."

"You can help me make decorations instead, Derek," Carter said, getting up and shoving paper and crayons into his arms.

"I didn't know you were an artist, Turner," Ben said with a chuckle.

"I'm not." Derek shrugged. "At least I can't burn anything while doing this. Though I'm not the one with the drawing skills."

He shot Maria a grin, but she only blushed in response, remembering the incident with her sketchbook.

He had come so close to seeing her drawing of him. Maybe she would show it to him one day.

No. She shook her head, walking to the kitchen to make sandwiches. He'd be gone before she built up the courage to show him her perception of him on paper.

Carter and Derek had transformed the atmosphere by the time she had prepared sandwiches, a bowl of fruit and a bowl of crackers, then set them out on a blanket in the living room. Even Ben helped.

They had cut out animal shapes from a roll of paper that Mary had, then colored them in and made paper vines that they taped to the walls and ceiling.

Carter watched his mother's reaction, obviously proud of his work. "What do you think? Welcome to our African jungle safari picnic!"

The funny part was that she could not tell Carter's drawings from Derek's.

"You don't have to tell me that my artistic talent rocks. I know," Derek said sarcastically, laughing.

"I wouldn't exactly say that it rocks. I could think of a few other ways to describe it." She held back a giggle and brought out some drinks to complete the picnic.

They sat down, and as Carter prayed for the food, she couldn't help but think how sweet it was for Derek to help Carter with decorating the living room. Coloring giant paper elephants, snakes and vines were definitely not part of his job description. But he had been happy to do it anyway. It was obvious how much he cared about Carter.

That evening, Maria put Carter to bed after finishing the chores and playing games in the living room.

"The picnic today was fun. It was better than having it outside," Carter said as she tucked him in, his face illuminated by a battery-operated light on his nightstand.

"It was fun. I'm sorry we can't go anywhere."

"It's okay. I know it's not safe to go places."

She smiled at his perceptiveness.

"Goodnight, baby. Sleep well." She kissed him on the forehead.

"Goodnight, Mommy."

She closed the door and went out into the living room. She didn't have the heart to take down his decorations, so she left them up.

Derek sat at the kitchen table. He was taking the first shift, and Ben was in bed already.

"Thanks for helping him with the artwork today," she said as she approached him.

"Really, it was fun. Even though I can't draw a stick figure. Actually, he drew the animals and stuff. I just colored them in."

"Oh. That's why they all looked like his drawings." She chuckled and sat down across from him.

"Yeah. I didn't want to ruin his fun. I let him do the hard stuff." He smiled at her in the dim light. "He's a really good kid. Smart. You should be proud of him."

"Thanks. He really is. I don't know where he gets all his perceptiveness from," she said with a sigh, leaning back. "Well, I guess his father was like that."

"Maybe he gets it from you. Ever thought of that?"

He didn't seem to try to hide the admiration in his voice.

She got up, feeling a little uncomfortable. She walked past him to get a drink of water and noticed black ink on the back of his upper arm poking out from under the short sleeve of his shirt.

"What's your tattoo of?" She filled a glass from the sink and leaned against the counter as she drank.

"It's a list of initials of all my friends who were killed in action. It started with just being Danny's initials, but after that I kept on adding to it. There's also their dates of birth and death."

Maria didn't ask to see it, but he tugged on the sleeve of his shirt so she could see, revealing a simple list of letters and numbers. Just a few markings that meant so much to Derek, more than she could ever understand.

She didn't know which was worse: enduring the death of a spouse or seeing several of your friends die while protecting their country. Maria couldn't even imagine the horrors of war that this man had witnessed. She didn't want to think about it.

166

"I think it's nice that you did that in their memory." She took her glass and sat down.

"I never thought I would get a tattoo. But I had to keep their memory alive somehow. Danny was engaged, you know."

A noise sounded on the front porch.

"What was that?" Derek was already up and walking toward the sound.

"Probably *Maam's* obnoxious cat. It's always chasing rodents and knocking the flower pots over." Maria shook her head and took a sip of her water.

Derek held up a hand, drew his gun, and slowly opened the front door.

Maria's smile fell, her pulse spiking. A silhouette slid over the window. A silhouette too large to belong to a cat.

The door flung open. Maria screamed as two masked intruders stormed inside and tried to take Derek down.

Derek swung at one of the men a few times and got in a few good punches, but the man wouldn't go down. Ben came running down the hallway and joined the fight. The four of them grappled for a few moments, then one of the intruders' guns crashed into Derek's skull. Derek fell to the floor, unconscious. The man grabbed Derek's weapon.

Ben took on the two men, but one of them broke away from the fight to charge toward Maria. His eyes found hers, daring her to move.

Carter was only a few doors down the hall. Her blood chilled, all reason fleeing her brain.

How can I fight him? she wondered. *What can I do?*

Maria smashed her glass on the table, then flung the shards into his eyes in a scooping motion. The man cried out, clawing at his eyes. The distraction gave her the second she needed to run down the hall, slipping and sliding in her socks.

Her only thoughts were of Carter.

She stopped at Derek's bedroom door, reached in and locked it, then slammed it shut from the outside. Heart hammering, she darted into Carter's room and left the door ajar to confuse the man.

Carter was trembling under the bed, and she realized she was also trembling herself. Maria bent down and motioned for him to be quiet. He nodded, then she motioned for him to follow her. The boy slid out from under the bed and stood near her as she opened the window quietly.

The intruder barreled down the hallway and fell for her trick, pounding on Derek's door even though the room was empty. She heard a banging noise come from the direction of the front door. Was Ben still fighting the other attacker?

"You open this door or I'll kick it down!" the man screamed, trying to open it with the force of running into it. He then resorted to kicking it open. But Gideon's craftsmanship was sturdy and strong, and it was going to take a few tries to bust it open.

168

As Maria opened the window in Carter's room, she heard the man break down the door and search the room.

"Where are you hiding?" he demanded, and she pictured him looking under the bed or in the closet.

Meanwhile, Maria climbed out the window. She helped Carter down, who bravely didn't make a sound. She quickly closed the window so it wasn't obvious how they had escaped. They tore off into the darkness, even though Maria had no idea where to go. She grabbed Carter's hand and veered toward the woods. On the way, she passed Sid Hoffman's house, who was outside on his front porch.

"Derek needs medical help! Two attackers came in and knocked him out," Maria cried as she ran by. "Tell him we are going to hide in the woods. Go!"

Sid hollered, "I will!" and ran towards a neighbor's house.

Knowing the woods inside and out would come to her advantage. They would hide and wait out the attackers.

As they entered the refuge of the trees, Maria whispered prayers for Derek and Ben.

"Please, God, wake him up. Keep them safe. Don't let those men hurt them," she begged, pulling Carter deeper into the woods. Guilt assailed her at the thought of leaving them there, but she knew she was doing what they would have wanted her to do.

Once they were out of earshot and far enough away from the house, Maria ducked behind a large patch of bushes and trees with

Carter. "Are you okay, baby? You were so brave and quiet. If you had cried or spoken, that man might have found us."

Carter burst into tears, the fear finally catching up with him. "What happened, Mommy? Who were those men? Did they want to hurt us?"

He threw his short arms around her neck, and she hugged him tightly, rubbing his back, like she used to do when he was a baby. "I don't know who they were. I don't know what they wanted to do to us."

"Where are Ben and Derek? Derek promised not to let those men hurt us!"

"Derek was hurt. He couldn't help. Ben tried to help, but I don't know what happened because I left to get you out of the house. That's why I took you out the window." She sent up another prayer for her bodyguards, and hoped Derek would wake up soon so he could help Ben arrest those men.

CHAPTER TWELVE

Derek's eyes slowly opened to see a sideways view of the kitchen and living room. Why was he on the floor? His ears rang, and his thoughts muddled together. What had happened?

The memories came rushing back like a tornado. The masked men had hit him in the head and gone after Maria. At the thought of her and Carter in danger, he sat straight up.

Lord, please protect them, he prayed.

Derek's head began pounding and he rubbed it. But he didn't have time to think about how dizzy he felt. He stood and staggered into the hallway, sometimes leaning against the wall for support. Ben was on the floor in the hall, unconscious.

Derek heard shuffling coming from his bedroom. He reached for his gun, but his holster was empty. One of the intruders must have swiped it from him. He'd have to fight unarmed.

He stormed into the room, taking the criminal by surprise and tackling him to the floor. There was only one of them. Had the other one taken Maria and Carter?

They grappled and punched at each other.

Derek reached for his own gun in the man's belt, but the criminal wrenched it from his hands before he could use it. He dropped it, and the intruder kicked it across the room.

The stalker then pulled out his own gun and aimed it at Derek, but Derek knocked it away. Derek lunged at him, knocking him to the floor and pinning him down. He tore at the man's mask, trying to yank it off.

"What's your name? Who do you work for?" Derek demanded.

He got the mask halfway off when searing electric pain shot into his side, then coursed through his body, immobilizing him. His body stiffened and he lost the ability to move, but he remained completely aware of what was happening.

He fell on the floor, feeling useless. He got a glimpse of the stun gun before the man opened the bedroom window and jumped out.

Voices sounded in the distance, but Derek wasn't sure if he was imagining it or not. The room spun and his ears rang, his head throbbing in pain as stars blinked across the room.

Had Maria and Carter escaped, or had they been taken? Derek willed himself to get up off the floor, but his limbs felt as though they were superglued to the floor, and his head felt as though it weighed as much as a block of cement.

The voices grew louder, and now Derek knew it wasn't his imagination. Several Amish men entered the room in a frenzy, all asking questions.

Sid Hoffman bent down and helped Derek sit up, and some of the other men ran to Ben. "Maria told me you needed help and then said she was going to hide in the woods. I rounded up the men and we came right away. What happened? Are you hurt?"

Derek rubbed his temple and took Sid's hands as he slowly sat up. "The stalker broke in, looking for Maria. I guess she got away somehow with Carter. I don't know where they are. Don't worry about us. Go find them." His words slurred together.

Derek clutched his head where he'd been hit with the gun and his side where he'd been electrocuted. It sure hurt, but he'd had injuries far worse than this. He wouldn't even think of getting medical attention until Maria and Carter were safe. Sid helped him up, and they went outside, searching for Maria and her son.

"Please, God, if you'll hear my prayer, please keep them safe," Derek whispered into the darkness. "Not for me, but for their sakes."

***

Several minutes had passed, and though the intruders were hopefully gone, Maria was too afraid to budge from her hiding spot. When she heard voices from her community calling her name, she hoped it was safe to come out now.

"Is it safe now?" Carter whispered, hanging onto her. "If they are outside, it must mean that the man is gone."

That's what she had been thinking. "I think so." She looked around. The woods were absolutely still.

"Maria?" several voices called from the fields. Maybe they'd scared the stalker off by now.

"You can come out now!" someone called. That sounded like Mrs. Johnson.

"Let's go," she said, taking Carter's hand and leading him out of the woods. Once they were out in the open, several of her neighbors ran to greet them.

"Are you all right? What happened?" someone asked, and several other questions followed.

Derek made his way through the group of people, and she realized it had been his voice that she had heard. A large bump and bruise had formed on his head, which he was rubbing.

"We're fine. I threw the intruder off by locking your bedroom door and making him think I was in there. Then I escaped with Carter through his bedroom window." She wanted to apologize for not going after him, but she would do that later when there wasn't anyone else around.

"You okay, buddy?" Derek asked Carter, putting a hand on his small shoulder.

"Yes, but that was scary!" Carter's eyes brimmed with tears again, and he clung to Maria as if the memories had suddenly flooded back to him.

"I know. I'm sorry, but that man knocked me down and I couldn't get up. And now Ben is unconscious, but I think he'll be fine." He rubbed his head again. "Sorry that happened, Carter."

"It wasn't your fault. It's okay," he said softly, then flung his arms around Derek's waist. At first, Derek was clearly surprised, then he hugged the boy back, smiling at Maria. She couldn't help but smile back, thankful that they were all safe.

"Thank you, Lord, for answering my prayers," she whispered. She looked at the crowd that had gathered around. "We are all fine. Thank you for your help."

***

At that, several of them nodded or murmured encouraging words, then everyone returned to their homes. Derek, Maria, and Carter walked back to the house, and Maria took her son to his room and tucked him in.

Derek heard their hushed voices from the kitchen, and he found himself walking toward the sounds. He stood outside the door, listening.

"I don't know if I will be able to sleep, Mommy. I'm afraid that bad man who came in my room will come back. I keep seeing him in my head when I close my eyes," Carter said in a small voice, and Derek imagined him pulling the covers up to his chin.

"Derek will protect us, baby. God will protect us. We are all right here, watching over you. You don't have to be afraid," Maria told him softly.

"But Derek and Ben couldn't stop him."

"I know, sweetie."

"I like Derek and Ben, especially Derek. When they catch the bad men, will Derek go away forever?"

Derek heard a pause and shuffling, as if Maria was situating herself closer to her son as she sat on the bed, maybe to stroke his hair. "Yes, baby. He has to go protect other people like us after he catches the bad men. Other people will need him, and we won't need him anymore."

Sadness welled up in the boy's voice, and it nearly broke Derek's heart. "But Derek is my friend. I will really miss him. Can he visit us?"

"I don't think so, sweetie. He will be very busy with his job."

Carter sniffled, and the bed sheets shuffled again. "It's okay. We should share him with other people. Can you read me a story?"

"Sure. One story." Maria walked across the room to get a book, then sat back down on the bed.

Derek couldn't help but peek around the corner to see her snuggled up next to her sweet son, reading a book to him. Longing filled his heart. He wanted children to play with and nurture and a wife to love, but it seemed impossible.

He didn't have much time for even his friends, so how would he have time to spend with his family? Besides, his job was dangerous, and there was the possibility every day that he might not come home.

Derek took another quick glance at Maria sharing a sweet moment with her son, envying their bond. Even the Amish way of life appealed to him—the simple, slow-paced lifestyle and their unwavering faith in the Lord that he envied so much.

He leaned against the wall. Could his relationship with God ever be that strong again, like it used to be? He wanted it more than anything.

Derek also admired the strong sense of community here that was so opposite from the life he knew, which was so full of violence and chaos.

Would he ever know the peace they had that was so normal to them?

Derek heard Maria kiss Carter, and the blankets rustled as she probably finished tucking him in.

Suddenly feeling as though he was intruding on something that he had no business witnessing, Derek walked back to the kitchen.

***

Once Maria settled Carter down and put him back to bed, she met Derek in the kitchen at his usual spot by the table. But this time, he held ice wrapped in a towel to his head. Ben had woken up and now sat next to him with a first aid kit on the table. He had a black eye and a gash on his forehead.

"You two look like you've seen better days," she said, getting a towel damp for Ben's forehead and handing it to him.

"Thanks," Ben said. "But actually, I'm just going to take a shower." He got up and hobbled to the bathroom.

"That's a pretty nasty bump you got there," she said, gently taking hold of Derek's hand and moving it aside so she could see the injury. She ignored the way his strong hand felt in hers, the way her pulse jumped in response to his touch. "My friend Anna should look at it. She's learning to be a midwife. She might know a thing or two about head injuries."

"I've had a lot worse than this. I'll be fine." He growled, replacing the ice.

"It could be a concussion."

"Nonsense. Don't worry about me."

She put her hands on her hips, staring at him stubbornly. "Please, just let me have her stop by tomorrow. It's the least I can do. Do it for my sake. So I don't worry about you." That had come out wrong. She hadn't meant to make it sound like she actually cared for him. But she didn't know what to say to correct it.

"Okay, fine, if it makes you feel better," he said, his tone softening.

"Good. We don't want it affecting your job." A bit of resentment laced the last two words, but it was so subtle that Derek didn't seem to notice. She hadn't meant to let her emotions show. But she was failing at hiding them lately, especially when she was around Derek.

"I'm sorry I didn't come for you before we ran." She sat down next to him. "I just had to get Carter out of there, and we only had a few seconds. Besides, I would have had to run by the man in order to get to you."

"Don't apologize. You did what you had to do to protect your son. Actually, I am very impressed at how quickly you reacted and how you tricked him into thinking you were in the other room by shutting and locking the door." He shifted in his chair to face her. She realized how close they were, and her breath caught in her throat. He was giving her that look again, filled with admiration, which baffled her beyond reason.

"Thanks," came her delayed response. His eyes were distracting her, the way their darkness sparkled in the moonlight, the way she could hear him breathing one chair away. She leaned back in her chair to put a few more inches between them. "I guess running from an abusive man has taught me to react quickly. My son's safety always comes first."

"I know. I really like that about you. You always put him first."

Confusion erupted in her brain. He liked that about her? Could his mixed signals get any worse? It perplexed her so much that it made her head hurt.

He lowered his ice and sagged in his chair. "I really failed tonight. If it wasn't for your quick thinking, you might be gone right now."

"They knocked you out. How is that your fault?" She instinctively brought her hand up to his head injury, feeling the bump swelling under her fingers.

Maria winced. That had to hurt. He took her hand, gently moving it away from the bump. She let her hand fall back into her lap. She'd gone too far. Embarrassment welled up inside her at her impulsive action.

"I shouldn't have let them get that close. Or in the house, for that matter. I'm really just not doing my job as well as I usually do. I've been so distracted, and I never get distracted," he admitted solemnly, looking away.

She furrowed her brow. "Distracted by what?"

Was this the reason why he wanted to leave? Perhaps something was going on in his personal life?

Derek wouldn't meet her eyes for several moments. Then he looked up, his dark eyes searching hers. Her heart pounded in her ears, her chest. She felt as if she was floating, suspended in a world of questions and the possibility of loving someone again, the one thing she thought she would never do.

"You. I was distracted by you, Maria."

Derek put the ice on the table and turned to face her in the chair. He leaned forward on his elbows, looking up into her face. His dark hair was disheveled, and his glasses were a little crooked.

Derek reached for her hand, and she forgot how to move as she let him hold it in his own. She should be pulling away, but she was afraid that if she even breathed, the moment would shatter.

"Ever since we met in that bank, I have been captivated by everything about you. I'm amazed at how you escaped your ex, the way you are raising Carter on your own and protect him no matter the cost, and the way you would sacrifice your own life for your family. That's why I failed to look for a tracker on your phone, why I requested a replacement, and that's why I'm not on my game. I've never deeply cared about a client before. Not like this."

Finally, her wits came back to her. She pulled her hand back and stood up, unable to bear his closeness a second longer. It permeated her entire being, messing with her head and quickening her heartbeat, distorting her judgment. He was her bodyguard, not her boyfriend.

"But there was no replacement available except a few rookies, and I couldn't stand the thought of a newbie being responsible for your safety. So I decided to stay. I vowed to myself to do better and be the best bodyguard that I could be for you. But I failed tonight, again. I'm so sorry."

Her head spun at his confession, and she leaned against the countertop for support. So that's why he had begged to leave. He did have feelings for her after all. What did he expect her to do? Fall into his arms and profess her love for him?

They both knew it could never work. She was Amish now. Carter needed a stable home environment, which he had with Mary and Gideon.

"You said yourself that you could do your job better without loved ones. Because your job is so dangerous," she told him firmly. "I don't understand what you expect me to say."

"I know. That's true. My job puts anyone I care about at risk." Now he was standing, coming closer to her. She wanted to run from him, yet she also wanted to run to him, to let him hold her like he had for that brief moment in the barn. To inhale his masculine, woodsy, and spicy scent, to finally feel completely safe.

And totally, irrevocably, wholly loved.

But that was a fantasy, one that would end in heartbreak when Derek realized he couldn't continue doing his job without putting them in danger. Then Carter's father figure would be ripped away again, and they would all be devastated.

"I could lose my job for this. This is completely against protocol." He came even closer, if that was possible, and let his hand reach up to gently touch her face. Not even Robert had ever made such a romantic gesture, and though it felt as though she was moving through wet cement, she pulled away from him.

"Then you shouldn't do this. Whatever this is," she retorted, stepping around him and walking to the other side of the table. She willed her heart rate to slow, trying to tamp down the warmth that had filled her chest at his touch. "This would never work out. I'm Amish, you're not. Your job would put us in danger. When he fully realizes that, Carter will be devastated. He really likes you, and I think you've grown close enough to him as it is. From the way he talks to me about you, he obviously thinks very highly of you. The truth is, we probably won't see you again after your job here is over. That alone will crush him."

His head dropped. "I'm sorry, Maria." He let out a heavy sigh. "You're right. You're totally right. I know that. But I just can't fight what I feel. I can usually fight off several armed men at once. I fought terrorists in the desert and have fought back shooting assassins in order to protect US senators. But I can't fight my feelings for you, Maria. And I don't want to fight them."

"If things were different..." she murmured, letting him walk closer to her again.

"If things were different, I'd tell you I was falling in love with you," Derek whispered, standing inches away from her.

All was silent except the sound of his breathing. She held her breath, the effect of his closeness freezing every muscle in her body.

"Forget protocol." Derek's eyes dropped to her lips, and his words floated over her softly like a weak summer breeze, shattering all the intentions of walking away that she'd had a moment ago.

She finally breathed in, realization and anticipation pumping through her veins. She shouldn't let him kiss her. This was going too far. What if the stalker came back? What if Derek couldn't do his job because he was distracted and someone got hurt?

But when he leaned in to her, all questions fled her brain and she let herself give in. She ran her hand down his toned arm, over the tattoo of his fallen friends, wanting to know the name of everyone on that list and their stories. She wanted to know everything about Derek. All his untold secrets that lurked in his dark eyes, even the terrible things he had endured on his tours of service.

Everything. All his stories and memories. The imperfect, the gruesome, the beautiful.

He wrapped his arm around her waist and pulled her closer. "You are the bravest woman I have ever met."

She closed her eyes, smiling a little as a delightful emotion filled her. If she didn't know any better, she would say it was love.

"Hey... Are we out of toilet paper?" Ben called from the bathroom. "Because I can't find any in here."

Her eyes shot open and reality fell on her like several bales of hay. "I'm sorry," she blurted, not really knowing exactly what she was sorry for, and made herself pull away, leaving Derek standing there with disappointment all over his handsome face.

"There should be some under the sink," Maria said, walking down the hall to the bathroom.

"Uh... I don't see any."

"I'll go get some downstairs then."

She sighed as she went into the basement to the storage area. That had been close. She had almost given into something that would have ended in heartbreak for her and her son. Carter came first. Always. She would not begin a fleeting summer romance that could only end in disaster. Because when the break up finally came, she would not be the only one who was hurt. Carter would be hurt just as much, if not more.

CHAPTER THIRTEEN

The next day dawned brightly like a newly made promise, and Maria went out to her phone shanty to call Anna on her cell phone. Since she was a midwife in training, Anna was allowed to have a cell phone for when pregnant women needed to call her. Maria didn't use her cell phone, since it was only meant for emergencies.

When she came back into the house, Derek was drinking a cup of coffee in the front doorway.

"You went outside without telling me or Ben?" he asked, a hint of worry coming through in his voice.

"I only went to the phone shanty. It's right there." Maria jabbed a thumb at the small shed down the lane. "I knew you'd be watching me." She brushed past him and went into the kitchen to make breakfast, awkwardness thick in the air like humidity. "Anna will stop by later when she has time."

Derek was silent except his footsteps as he walked up behind her, but this time he gave her space. His voice dropped low. "Maria, I'm so sorry about last night. I was extremely unprofessional and impulsive."

Her heart raced and her face heated at the memories of the night before, of their almost-kiss. She couldn't deny that she had spent hours reliving those moments as she tossed and turned in her bed, too confused to sleep. The way he had pulled her toward him, how he had held her close, tipping his face nearer to hers...

Then how Ben had ruined the moment.

How she wished that they had actually kissed. She wondered over and over how his lips would have felt on hers.

She set a pan on the wood stove with a little more force than necessary, the slam of cast iron interrupting her thoughts. "I'm sorry, too."

"That we didn't kiss? Or for walking away?"

Both, she thought.

"I'm sorry I let it go that far." She ignored the way his closeness made her feel as she busied herself with cooking eggs and making toast in a pan on the wood stove.

"It won't happen again if you don't want it to."

Maria spun around to face him. "Honestly, that's not it. I would love it if it happened again." She surprised herself at how she had let the words tumble out of her mouth, but she continued. "You said yourself that with your job it's dangerous to have people in your life you are close to. I just don't want to start something that we both know can't be long term. It would break Carter's heart to lose you after growing even closer to you. Besides, I'm Amish and you're not. I'd be shunned. I'm pretty sure that you're not too keen on becoming Amish yourself." She sighed. "See my point?"

"Maria, I do understand. I'll just do my job. There will be no repeat of last night. When my job here is over, if you want me to leave you alone, I will. Does that sound fair?" He looked her in the eye, his voice deep and soft.

"That sounds fair."

"Good morning," Ben said, walking in to the kitchen. "That smells delicious."

"Good morning, Ben," Maria said.

Her heart wrenched at the thought of Derek leaving, but she knew it was inevitable. She had gotten over the loss of her husband, the one man she had loved truly and deeply. Surely she would be able to get over this sort of summer fling with her too-good-to-be-true bodyguard. She had endured worse heartaches.

After breakfast and the morning chores, Anna stopped by to look at Derek and Ben's injuries.

"If you have any of these symptoms within the next few days, you need to go to the hospital," she said, passing Derek a handwritten list of symptoms. Then she turned to Ben and examined his cut.

Maria smiled as she watched them talk. Anna and Ben seemed to be hitting it off right away. A few minutes later, Anna finished up.

"Thank you so much for coming, Anna. I know your schedule is very busy these days," Maria said, walking Anna to the door.

"It's really no problem. It keeps me busy. Keeps my mind off things." She chuckled humorlessly.

188

"What do you mean?"

"I know Simon loves me, but something doesn't feel quite right. I don't think I love him nearly as much as he loves me. He's such a great guy though. I just don't know if he's the one."

"There is a wonderful man somewhere out there for you. God will bring him to you at the right time. Don't worry," Maria said, resting a hand on her friend's shoulder.

"You're probably right. Speaking of wonderful men." Her eyebrows wiggled and she dropped her voice to a whisper, grinning. "Your bodyguards are terribly handsome. Not to mention buff. Especially Ben. He's quite nice, isn't he?" Anna blushed again.

"Anna!" Maria smacked Anna playfully on the arm.

"What? Just saying! As if you hadn't noticed!" She giggled, gathering up her things and opening the front door. "Too bad they're both *Englishers*."

Maria laughed out loud as they walked onto the porch. "Oh, Anna. We were both taught that outward appearances don't matter. It's what's inside that counts."

"But good looks sure are a bonus, and they've both got them. See you later, Maria!" Anna called, waving as she got in her buggy and drove away.

Maria walked back into the house, laughing to herself at her silly friend's words. Derek leaned up against the table and Ben stood near him, both smiling mischievously. Her cheeks instantly heated up.

"You heard that, didn't you?" she asked, her stomach freefalling.

"We heard enough." Derek laughed. "Your friend is very lively."

She laughed nervously. "Sorry. She's funny like that."

"I'm flattered. She called us handsome and buff," Ben said, jabbing Derek in the ribs with his elbow. "But I'm pretty sure she was mostly referring to me." His joking tone didn't calm her embarrassment, but at least it lightened the mood.

"I've got to go feed the cats in the barn. I'll be right back," she said, mostly to change the subject.

"Not alone. I'll come with you," Ben said.

It was only the barn, but she didn't bother arguing.

"I want to come too!" Carter called from the hallway. He slid down the hall and put on his shoes. His excitement from seeing the farm animals was not even close to fading.

"Well, then, I guess we are all going," Derek said.

As they entered the barn, Maria realized she had grown to really appreciate the smell of hay and horses. She didn't even mind the manure. Those smells meant she was home.

She poured cat food and water into the cats' bowls and was interrupted when Ben called her over. "Look at this."

A note was folded on a bale of hay. Derek picked it up, only touching the corners, though there probably weren't any prints on it. He had dusted the last ones himself with his fingerprint kit and the only prints on it had been his own on the very edges. Derek read it, then showed it to Maria.

You told me you don't know anything, but I don't believe you. Your ex must have told you something. He was quite the talker. Come forward or I will start taking Amish girls one by one until you give yourself up.

Maria could feel the color drain from her face as they read the handwritten note. Now he was threatening her friends—girls and women she'd grown up with.

"What do we do?"

"That's enough. I don't care how the Amish feel about more of my guys coming here to patrol. We need the backup now before anyone goes missing." Derek whipped out his cell phone and called Branson to arrange having several officers come and patrol the community until further notice.

He was right. Her neighbors definitely wouldn't like police sitting and driving around in their cop cars, but it would be for their own safety.

Derek hung up his phone. "We've got to catch this gang before they do anything else. That's all there is to it," he muttered. "I have to go see if there are any prints on this. Let's go inside."

They had only taken a few steps from outside the barn to the house when they heard a high-pitched scream coming from down the lane.

The lane Anna had just gone down only a few minutes before on her way home.

"Anna!" Maria screamed and started running.

***

Derek caught up to her in a few long strides and grabbed her arm to stop her. "No. You go in the house with Ben and lock yourself and Carter in a room until I come back. Go now!" He sprinted down the dirt road, stuffing the note into his pocket while Ben hurried Maria and Carter into the house.

Derek ran with ferocity toward the screams, his heart pounding in his ears. He prayed he wouldn't be too late.

He reached the buggy. The horse whinnied and stomped the ground, flustered.

"Anna? Anna!" he shouted, then looked inside the buggy. Anna's medical bag and cell phone were in the passenger's seat, but other than that, it was empty.

She was gone.

As he called Branson on his cell phone, demanding that the backup come immediately, he searched the ground for tracks or any other clues. The only marks on the road were from the wheels on a buggy. There were some footprints that looked like they belonged to Anna that lead to the side of the road, but there was not another set. That meant that the kidnapper had lured Anna to stop and come out of her buggy before he had taken her. Had he been dressed like an Amish man? Had he asked her for help with something? Perhaps a fake injury if he had known she had medical training? If he did, that meant he had been watching her.

Anger coursed through Derek's veins. He just couldn't wait to get his hands on this guy who preyed on innocent young women.

Derek dashed into the woods that lined the edge of the road and listened carefully. They could have gone in any direction. Or he could have stuffed her in another buggy, if he had one, and driven off so his tracks would blend in with the wheel marks of the other buggies. It was rare to see the tire marks of a car on these lanes.

As he stood in the woods, he felt utterly helpless.

"Somehow, God, let me find her," he whispered.

After several minutes of searching, he gave up. Defeated, he decided to wait until his men arrived to help. He needed to check on Maria and Carter.

When he entered the house, he found them locked in Carter's room.

"What happened? Did you find her?" Maria asked, but he could tell by the look on her face that she knew the answer was no. He slowly shook his head.

She bit her lip in an effort to hold back the tears, but her lip quivered and a few tears escaped down her cheeks. His heart hurt for her. He had disappointed her. He hated the feeling. All he wanted to do was wrap her in his arms and promise her that it would be okay, and that he would find her friend and find the criminal.

Against his better judgment, his arms raised as if invisible strings pulled them, and Maria ran into them. She let out a sob and cried into his chest, clutching onto his linen shirt. The shirt that had belonged to her husband. But he didn't care about that.

Ben turned away to give them a moment. He rubbed her upper back a few times reassuringly, but he wanted to kiss all her tears away. He told her he was sorry, but he wanted to remove her head covering and run his fingers through her long hair.

"Mom? What happened to Anna?"

All too soon Maria stepped away. She knelt down in front of Carter. "Anna is gone away. But Derek, Ben, and their coworkers are going to try to find her."

"Did the bad man take her?"

"Honey, why don't you go play in the living room with Ben? I'll be right there."

"Okay, Mom." Carter walked slowly out of the room with Ben.

She turned to Derek, blushing. "I'm sorry for crying on you like that. It's just that she is one of my dearest friends. If anything happens to her because of me—" A new round of tears came, and she sniffled. "I couldn't live with myself. We have to do something."

"Men from CPDU will be here soon. We will patrol the community day and night, and we will find her." He knew that after

24 hours the chances of finding her alive would dramatically decrease with every hour. "We will find her, Maria, I promise," he said, then instantly regretted it. He had no business making promises like that. She could already be dead for all he knew.

But when he saw those big brown eyes fill with tears, he just couldn't help it.

His phone vibrated, announcing the arrival of his coworkers who were in unmarked cop cars, wearing plainclothes that resembled Amish clothing close enough. He filled them in on the situation over the phone, so that the stalker would not see them meet and become aware of the cops' presence in the community.

There had been no witnesses to the abduction. Derek went to Anna's parents' house, but they didn't seem to know anything. So, CPDU didn't have much to go on.

Police were scattered across the community, walking around, camouflaged in clothing similar to what Amish men wore, watching and waiting for any sign of the kidnappers' return.

Hopefully, the stalkers had no idea that the police were there, but these men were smart. Were they keeping track of who came and went within the community? Would they notice these newcomers?

They had threatened to kidnap several Amish girls, so they would most likely be back to carry out their threats.

And Derek would be ready for them.

CHAPTER FOURTEEN

In the morning, Maria sat straight up in bed, sucking in air as if she had been underwater. But it had only been a dream. She had seen Anna running from the masked man, but he had overtaken her. No matter how hard she fought, he only became stronger. She couldn't escape.

Maria grabbed her Bible off her nightstand and prayed for her friend as the sun rose, tears wetting the worn pages of scripture. How many times had she cried over these pages? How many times had this book brought her comfort? She hated to admit it, but today, no matter how many Psalms she read, her heart still ached for her friend, and worry plagued her like a dark cloud.

She ambled to the kitchen where she started making breakfast.

Derek approached, his expression dark. "Another woman has been kidnapped."

Her heart dropped. "Who?"

"Liz Kulp," he said grimly. "I'm so sorry, Maria."

She covered her face with her hands. Liz was a girl Maria knew from church, a sweet teenager who loved reading. She had probably been reading outside or walking along the lane, or not paying attention while doing her chores.

"When?"

"Early this morning. Ben just got back from her house to question her parents. They said she was taken from her barn while feeding their animals. No one saw anything. This man leaves behind no evidence, no sign of a struggle. He knows what he's doing. The only reason anyone realized she was missing was because her mother went to look for her after not coming in from the barn."

Maria dropped her head. "Thank you for letting me know."

Derek nodded and walked down the hall.

She wondered how she could help the families. Bringing them a meal would be good, and offering them her assistance with whatever they needed in this difficult time. How must they be feeling right now? Maria was worried enough, but she was not even family.

And no matter how hard she tried, she could not shake the idea that this was all her fault. This man was here because of her, because she had gotten involved with Trevor—the worst mistake of her life.

She hurled her wooden spoon across the kitchen, letting out a growl of frustration. What had she been thinking, running off with a man she barely knew and a child to take care of? Her mistakes still haunted her years later, prowling around the farms and stealing the community's innocence.

She wanted to do something more than take their families meals, but what? What could she do that would even make a difference? It's not like she could bring the young women home.

Wait. Maybe she could somehow bait the kidnapper and the police could arrest him in the process, then question him to find out where he was keeping the young girls.

If they had not already been trafficked by now. The thought of the atrocities involved made her sick with worry and guilt, and she ran to the bathroom just in time before vomiting. She leaned against the bathroom wall, sliding slowly to the floor. What if they were already gone? What if they had already been transported somewhere?

She could barely process the word in her thoughts: *sold*. What if they had already been sold?

"Maria? Are you all right?" Derek asked outside the bathroom door.

She slid a sleeve over her mouth. "I'm fine."

"You don't sound fine."

She couldn't argue with him. She was literally worried sick for her friends. How many more would be taken before this man was arrested?

Pushing herself to her feet, she brushed her teeth and stood a few moments later. She needed some air. Gathering her wits enough to walk out the front door, she took several deep breaths of fresh country air.

"What are you doing?" Derek asked from the kitchen.

"Don't worry. I'm not going anywhere. Just getting some air." It helped her nausea subside, and she sat on the bench on the porch, letting her head fall in her hands.

"You okay?" Derek asked at the door.

"Not really, to be honest. The thought of what could be happening to my friends is making me sick." She looked up at him. "How do you do this job? How do you deal with seeing people in such horrific circumstances?"

"I wish I could say it gets easier. But it doesn't. But that's why I want to help people, protect people, and rescue people. Come inside. Drink some water. You'll be okay." He held out his hand, and she took it as he helped her up. They turned to the front door and stopped.

A white piece of folded paper was taped to the door. Derek snatched it up, unfolded it carefully and read it out loud.

"*Maria, meet me tonight at the old barn alone and unarmed at 8pm or see another friend go missing.*" Derek's hand shook a little in anger as he held the paper, as though he was resisting the urge to crumple up the note and hurl it off the porch.

There had to be something she could do to help her friends.

"I have an idea," she said as they walked into the kitchen.

"I don't like the sound of this already," Derek said, staring out the kitchen window over the fields.

"I can't stand by and watch while my friends are kidnapped one by one," she choked out, her throat constricting with grief. "I want to bait the kidnapper—or kidnappers."

"We can't let you do that," Ben said.

"Right. We were assigned to protect you, not get you killed. This is worse than your idea to meet the stalker in the barn," Derek argued, whirling around to face her. "I won't allow this."

"You have more officers to help you now. Just let me go out to the barn to meet them, and they can hide and watch. When they come to take me, CPDU can arrest them. It's one or two men against all of you."

Derek stared at her, his features softening just a little as he considered her words. "We don't know how many perps there are. There could be a whole group of them."

"These women who were taken are my friends. I have to help them somehow, and this is it."

A few seconds ticked by, and Derek let out a heavy breath. "I'll talk to my boss and my team about it. But I'm not promising anything."

"You promised that we would find Anna."

Derek bit his lip, guilty as charged. "I know. But this might not be the way."

"You got a better idea? You said yourself that these men are basically untraceable. They leave no evidence, nothing to track them with. This is the only way to get them to come out in the open so you can nab them. Don't you want to get these guys?" She threw her hands up, her voice rising with every word she spoke.

"Of course I do!" Derek blurted. "More than anything."

"Go call them right now. Please, let me do this! Let me help."

Ben looked at Derek and shrugged. Derek took a deep breath and dug his phone out of his pocket, walking into the living room to make the calls.

As she took out pans and eggs to make breakfast, a new feeling filled her, something she had not experienced in so long that she had forgotten what it felt like: hope.

***

"Good thing my parents aren't here," Maria muttered as she pulled on her shoes that night after a plan was formed with CPDU's undercover officers and agents. "They'd never let me do this. My mom would be a train wreck."

"I'm sure I hate this just as much as they would." Derek leaned against the entryway wall, arms crossed in disapproval. "I especially hate that Ben and I have to stay here, wondering what's going on the entire time so the stalker thinks you're alone."

"But at the same time of course we're happy to stay with Carter," Ben added.

"Really, I'll be fine. If your men are half as good as you say they are, they won't let anything happen to me. Just play with Carter, and we will be back before you know it." Maria said and stood.

"We are going to have fun!" Carter yelled, barreling around the corner. "Come on, Mr. Ben, let's pretend to be airplanes! Zoom!" Carter tugged on Ben's hand and they flew down the hallway. Maria smiled.

In a fleeting moment, Derek had eliminated the space between them. He stood close to her, gripping her upper arms gently. Her insides warmed at his touch, and though she knew she should move away, she couldn't.

"Please be careful out there," he whispered.

She nodded, left voiceless by his presence. His right hand rose to her face, where he ran a thumb along her cheek. For all she knew, this could be the last time she would ever see him.

He leaned closer, the gap between his lips and hers closing. She inhaled his woodsy scent, comforted by the familiarity of it. She wrapped her arms around him and tipped her head up, standing on her toes.

"Now let's play Go Fish!" Carter called, scrambling into the room with a giggle. He stopped to look at them, and they jumped apart as if lightning had zapped them. "What are you doing?" Carter tilted his head sideways in confusion.

Maria could feel her face blushing as she shook her head, chiding herself. What would Carter have done if he had seen them kiss? "Nothing. Come give me a hug, Carter. I'm just going to visit someone," Maria said, kneeling down and opening her arms to her son, who ran to her and hugged her. She held him tightly, breathing in his kiwi-scented hair, feeling its softness in her fingers. A lump grew in her throat, the fear finally kicking in as her eyes filled with tears. Maria squeezed him one last time and stood up. "Have fun. I'll be right back," she said, and turned to Derek. "Take care of my son."

"We will, Maria. You just worry about keeping yourself safe."

After looking at Derek one last time, Maria walked out the door, the image of his worried face filling her mind.

She could feel someone watching her as she walked down the porch steps and made her way to the barn. CPDU's people were hidden in the trees and walking around dressed in Amish clothing, all monitoring her every movement. Some even waited in the barn, lurking in the shadows, weapons cocked and ready. But she knew that the kidnappers were watching her, too.

What if something went wrong? What if someone got hurt? What if their plan failed, and the stalker—or stalkers—killed her or kidnapped her?

As her heartbeat pounded in her ears and her adrenaline surged, she thought of Derek, who was probably watching her, worrying about her, maybe even praying for her.

She walked on, moving one foot in front of the other, her anxiety mounting higher with every step. Gravel crunched under her shoes, the ordinary sound grating her nerves. The birdsong that usually made her smile did not comfort her today.

Maria approached the barn doors and grabbed onto the door handle, yanking it open before she could give it another thought. She worried about her friends, who must be terrified, homesick, and confused, maybe hungry or hurt. This was the only way to rescue them, and Maria would do it without considering her own fear a moment longer, because she knew it couldn't compare to theirs.

"I'm here!" she called out into the barn, her voice echoing off old timber beams and dusty corners.

Maria waited for movement, boots pounding on the old wooden floors, or the stalker's gravelly voice. There was nothing but the sound of her own frantic breathing. Perhaps he had seen the undercover agents and had decided not to show.

CHAPTER FIFTEEN

"Sorry we are eating so late, buddy," Derek said, staring in confusion at the directions on a box of macaroni and cheese. Different from normal Amish cuisine, but it was the best kind of food—and some of the only food—Derek could cook without burning the house down.

Maria had refused to eat, saying she was too anxious. Derek had been occupied with making plans with his team over the phone, and Carter had had an afternoon snack and wasn't hungry until now.

The water came to a boil and Derek dumped the entire contents of the box into the water.

"Oh, shoot!" he exclaimed, frowning at the pot, where a silver pouch was floating on the bubbles.

He let out a groan of frustration when he realized that he had not only dumped in the macaroni but the cheese pouch as well. He used a big spoon to fish it out. Letting out a long breath, he thought, *I really do need some cooking lessons.*

"What?" Carter said from the table, where he was coloring. "You didn't know you're supposed to take out the cheese *before* dumping in the macaroni?" He giggled. "That's silly."

"I just forgot." He plucked the cheese packet out of the boiling water by one of its corners and dropped it on the counter. "I told you I'm a terrible cook."

"Yeah, you are. Macaroni and cheese is supposed to be one of the easiest things to cook," Ben said from where he sat at the table next to Carter.

Carter gave a cheeky smile. Derek and Ben couldn't help but laugh. Growing up, Derek's mother had always cooked, and then Natalia had cooked for him. Since then, it had been easy microwave dinners with no water boiling involved. He could learn a thing or two from Maria, if she'd show him. Derek smiled at the thought of her giving him cooking lessons. It sounded like fun, if he didn't mess it up too badly.

"I've got to go to the bathroom." Carter climbed down from the table.

"I'll go with you and wait in the hall," Ben said.

"This should be ready in a few minutes, and then we can eat," Derek said, watching Carter amble down the hallway with Ben.

As the water boiled, Derek stared at the barn from out of the large window in the living room. What was happening out there? For the moment, all seemed peaceful. He wasn't sure if that was a good sign or a bad one.

He heard an odd noise and realized the water in the pot was boiling over onto the stove. Running over in a frenzy, he lowered the heat, then wiped the stove off.

After the timer beeped, he strained the pasta in a strainer over the sink, then returned it to the pan and added the cheese.

"It's ready!" he called, scooping it into bowls and grabbing three forks. He couldn't deny that this was one of his favorite foods, even if it was meant for kids. Hopefully, he hadn't messed it up too badly or overcooked it.

"Carter? Ben?"

The boy had been in the bathroom for a while now. What was taking so long? Was he trying to gel his hair like Derek or something? Derek started to walk toward the hall, then he heard a crashing noise on the porch.

Drawing his Glock 21 pistol, he hurried to the front door toward the noise. He crept up to the door and flung it open, gun raised. A flowerpot had been knocked over, and shards of pottery and dirt were strewn all over the porch.

He had a feeling Mary's cat hadn't knocked it over.

"Derek!" Ben cried from inside the house.

Derek darted back inside and bolted down the hall to see two masked men fighting Ben. They must have sneaked in through the back door while Derek was distracted.

"Where's the boy?" one demanded gruffly. Derek swung at him and punched him in the face, then tackled him to the floor while Ben fought the other intruder.

The man tried to grab Derek's gun, but Derek elbowed him in the face, then scrambled off him, standing up. The man went for his gun and aimed at Derek, so Derek shot him. A muffled pop filled the air as Derek's weapon fired, the sound suppressed by his silencer. The man was sprawled out on the floor, motionless.

Derek didn't have time to think about what he had just done. He helped Ben take down the other intruder, and they knocked him out, handcuffing him to the stair railing.

"Where's Carter?" Derek asked, trying to catch his breath.

"Thank goodness, he's still in the bathroom," Ben said, opening the door. "Carter? Everything is ok now. You can come out. Carter?"

"Carter!" Derek cried, barging into the bathroom.

It was empty, and the window was opened. A small step stool had been pushed up to the wall under the window.

"The fighting must have scared him," Ben said, voicing Derek's thoughts.

"He's probably looking for his mom. You stay here with these two, and I'll go get him. Hopefully we aren't too late." Derek climbed out the window and landed on the ground softly, then took off running toward the dilapidated barn at the end of the lane, wondering what was happening. If Maria was safe, and if Carter had already ruined the sting operation.

A small figure ran to the sagging structure, calling for his mother. Derek sprinted even faster.

***

"Mommy? The bad man is in the house!"

Maria froze when she heard Carter's voice crying out for her. What was he doing out here? What had happened to Ben and Derek? And how had they let Carter leave the house unnoticed? Had someone attacked Ben?

"Mommy!" Carter's voice changed from curious to completely terrified.

His voice ripped through the fields and into the barn, sending Maria running to the barn doors, desperate to see what was making him so afraid.

"It's the bad man, Mommy!"

Maria heard Carter's voice right before she broke out of the barn doors, then saw the masked stalker gripping her wriggling son with one arm and holding a gun to his head with another. The man wore a black mask that covered his whole face, and he wore Amish clothing.

"Don't hurt him!" she screamed, knowing all of the hidden officers and agents around her were watching, closing in.

"Make one wrong move and he dies!" the masked man shouted. "I know these fields and woods are crawling with undercover cops. My men have guns on every cop here. You all better slowly come out from hiding and drop your weapons or I'll shoot him. My men won't hesitate to shoot all of you cops either." He screamed louder, "Do it now or the boy's dead, and so are all of you!"

"Do what he says," the leader of the rescue team ordered from an unknown spot.

Several CPDU agents and police officers emerged from the long grass of the fields, from behind trees, and some came out of the barn, all camouflaged. Every one of them was followed closely by masked men carrying assault weapons. Maria watched in awe, shocked at the number of them.

Had Ben and Derek been this outnumbered the entire time?

All of the police slowly set their weapons on the ground at their feet, defeat shadowing their faces and slumped shoulders.

"Good." The attacker nodded. From behind him, Maria noticed Derek running toward them at full speed. She didn't know what the criminal would do if he saw Derek.

"Now. You are coming with me, missy," the man seethed, "and if you don't, I'll kill your son. But if you come with me, I'll let him go in the care of all these fine cops."

Maria looked to him, then to Carter's wide and terrified eyes. She looked to Derek, who was slowing down and staring at her. It was too far to clearly see his face, but she knew he was as scared as she was.

The man pulled back the hammer on his gun, and the sound of metal on metal might as well have been the sound of a guillotine. She had to go with him to save Carter. It was her only choice.

"I'll do as you say," she choked out, fear constricting her throat and tears blurring her vision. "Just let my son go."

"Walk to me slowly, and when I've got you, I'll let him go. He is of no use to me." She obviously didn't trust him, but she had no choice. For all she knew, she could go to him and he would shoot her son anyway or take him with them. But she had to try.

She walked toward him, feeling as though she was walking the plank straight to her death. Once she reached him, he grabbed hold of her and shoved Carter aside. He fell to the ground in front of a few of the cops, who helped him up.

"Mom!" he cried. "I'm sorry. There was another bad man in the house and I was scared." Tears soaked his pudgy cheeks, and Maria's heart broke.

"Baby, I love you. Listen to Derek and Ben. They'll protect you. And listen to your grandparents." Those were the only words she could get out before the man yanked her away, leading her to a horse and buggy parked a short distance down the lane. Had he kidnapped Anna in that same buggy?

But that was the last thing on her mind. Carter started to run after her, sobbing, but the police held him back. In a moment, Derek scooped up Carter to console him, looking as though he was about to weep himself.

She knew her parents would raise Carter as their own child. He would grow up Amish and live a wholesome life—but without her. Another sob wracked her body, and she wiped her face with her sleeve.

The man grabbed rope from the buggy and tied her hands behind her back. "If anyone follows me, she dies!" he shouted to the police.

He stuck a piece of duct tape over her mouth and shoved her into the buggy.

Dread and hopelessness covered her like a shroud as the rope cut into her wrists and her heart ached with sorrow. How would they ever find her? Most women were not ever found once sucked into human trafficking.

As the buggy lurched forward, the darkness of night settled over the land. Maria twisted around to look at her son and the man she loved for one last time, praying she would be one of the few who made it back home.

But she also doubted it.

***

Keep it together, Turner, Derek told himself as he watched Maria being taken away in the man's horse and buggy. He watched helplessly, feeling her slip away like sand through his fingers. Would he ever see her again? He wanted to fall to the ground and weep, to beg God to keep her alive and get her home somehow.

But that would take a miracle. He just wasn't sure if he believed in miracles anymore.

The other masked men slowly backed away, guns raised, then sprinted to a van that had been concealed in the trees. They piled in and started to drive away, but the CPDU officers took the opportunity to shoot out the tires and stop the van. The CPDU officers changed positions to new vantage points and hid themselves as they shot at the traffickers who emerged from the van, shooting back. Most of them went down, and the remaining were arrested for questioning.

Derek was already hiding behind the barn with Carter. He didn't want the boy to witness the violence. Derek swallowed away the lump in his throat. He blinked away hot tears as he held Carter close, who was sobbing into Derek's shoulder.

"It'll be okay, Carter," he told the boy, not believing his own words.

Derek came out of his hiding spot with Carter once all of the surviving traffickers were arrested and taken away in police vehicles. Several officers and agents were in the van, looking for anything that would help lead them to the trafficking headquarters.

"How are we supposed to rescue her without being able to follow her?" one of the officers asked. "It'll be impossible to track that buggy. They are all over the place and they all look exactly the same. They don't even have license plates. Besides, he probably didn't go far with it and switched to another vehicle as soon as he got far enough away."

Derek nodded to Carter, who was still crying, but most likely listening, indicating for the officer to stop discussing the subject in front of the child. He didn't want Carter to think there was no hope in finding his mother.

"I'm going to take Carter to the house so you can all work out a good plan to find Maria," he said in what he hoped sounded like a hopeful tone. Then he whispered to his men, "I don't want him hearing this. And I need an officer to come with me. There's a trafficker down and one is unconscious at the house."

It was just foolish to keep the boy's hopes up. His mother had just been sent into the equivalent of a dark void from which hardly anyone ever returned—the dark void of human trafficking. And even if she did return, she would probably not be the same person at all.

Derek took Carter back to the house with another officer, where the boy cried and cried in Derek's arms for what could have been ten minutes or ten hours while the surviving trafficker was arrested.

Derek wasn't sure how long Carter cried, but the longer the boy cried, the more guilt and sorrow weighed on Derek's heart. Time seemed to have lost its meaning. Nothing mattered except getting Maria home safely.

An impossible dream.

"I just wanted to get away from those bad men," Carter whimpered, sniffling and wiping his nose, rubbing his red eyes. "I just wanted my mommy."

"We know, Carter. It's not your fault. All you can do now is pray for your mom," Ben said, standing next to them with his arms crossed. "I'm really sorry for what happened, Agent Turner."

"There's nothing we can do about it now. Feeling sorry won't help things," Derek said. He looked up into his partner's eyes, seeing guilt and regret. "We did the best we could."

If only there was some way to reach Maria.

Her cell phone! Had she taken it with her?

"Hold on, Carter," Derek said, dashing down the basement stairs to see if it was charging in one of the few outlets.

When he saw that it wasn't there, he ran up to her room. He searched her bedroom, looking in her nightstand drawer and her closet. Then he searched her desk filled with her precisely sharpened pencils, but there was no cell phone.

He whirled around, knocking over her sketchbook in the process. It landed on the floor face down, and he picked it up to put it back. When he realized what was on the page, he froze, his heart stuttering.

His face filled the page. Maria's every stroke of pencil matched his features exactly, every smudge and shadow portraying him accurately. On the page beside it was a drawing of him and Maria walking down the lane, holding hands. He was wearing Amish clothing, and so was she. Radiant smiles graced their faces, their love for each other obvious in the way they were looking at each other.

So she did love him. A slow, vibrant smile spread across his face, and love for her coursed through him, the desire to rescue her and keep her safe so strong that it hurt.

He placed the sketchbook back on the desk. He would look through the rest later, hopefully with her.

Right now, he had to tell CPDU to track her cell phone's location.

CHAPTER SIXTEEN

"Stay down, and don't even think about trying anything," the masked man demanded. She reluctantly crouched in the back of the buggy as it began moving toward the end of the lane. Fear spiraled through her as her heart pounded, and she repeated one thought over and over again in her mind: *CPDU will find me. God, please let them find me.*

Wouldn't they, somehow?

The man pulled his mask off. With his shaggy hair, beard, and Amish clothing, he played the part of an Amish man well.

She continued praying every moment as the buggy jostled down the road. *God, please get me home safely,* she prayed. *Somehow, use me to help rescue the other girls.*

The man looked behind them for someone following them, then turned the buggy into the parking lot of an old abandoned gas station. He drove to the back, where a large white van with no rear windows waited. The buggy parked beside it, and the man exited, coming around to the back for her. His eyes scanned the parking lot for anyone watching, and he turned his cold eyes to her.

"Get in the van. Try anything, and I'll shoot you on the spot." He lifted the hem of his shirt to show her his gun tucked in his belt. Then he pulled her down, prodded her toward the van.

One of the men patted her down. Maria wasn't sure what he was looking for—maybe he was searching her for weapons. When he didn't find anything on her, he opened the back doors and threw her in.

It had happened so fast that she couldn't have signaled someone for help even if she tried. She blinked rapidly as her eyes adjusted to the dim light of the van. As her surroundings came into view, she realized she was sitting among several young women and teenage girls, all looking as terrified as she was. Some were crying, and some just stared off into space. Others looked around nervously. A sick feeling washed over Maria. What was going to happen to all of them?

Maria searched the faces for Anna and Liz, but they were not among the girls. She slid her tied hands under and over her legs so that her hands were now in front of her, and she ripped the duct tape off, wincing at the sting. But the pain was the last thing on her mind.

"What's going on? Where did you all come from?" she whispered. Several of them just stared at her, their eyes looking empty and lifeless as if they had lost every shred of hope they had been clinging to. Maria's heart sank even lower, if that was even possible.

One girl looked around, then spoke up when she concluded no one was going to speak. "I don't know about anyone else, but I was taken from the Maine Mall today. There was this guy I met who was really hot and really nice to me, and we were hanging out all day. I thought we were friends. Actually, I thought he liked me. He seemed sweet. He offered to take me to a movie, but instead he drove me to the back of a building where this van was. He threatened me with a knife and made me get in." The girl, who looked about sixteen, dropped her head and began to sob. "I can't believe I fell for it all. I'm so scared."

Maria's heart broke for her and every other girl and woman in the van. "Did you see any other young Amish women? They wear dresses and bonnets like me. There were two that were taken from my community." Some of them shook their heads. She dropped her voice as low as possible. "I'm going to try to get us out of here."

"There's no point, you naïve Amish girl," came a quiet voice from the front of the van. "They'll catch you, and you'll wish you wouldn't have tried." A girl with dark hair and dark circles under her eyes spoke, her voice flat. "You might as well give up any hope you have of escaping now."

"Aren't the police looking for us?" Maria demanded. "Especially because of all the other kidnappings in the area?"

"Of course," the girl said. "But haven't you ever heard that trafficked people aren't usually found? There's no use in hoping to be rescued. These guys are going to make us disappear. It's what they do."

A few sniffles and whimpers sounded from the other girls.

"Can't we try to escape then?" Maria said. "Maybe we can if we all work together. Isn't there anything we can do?"

"As I said," said the girl with the dark hair, "if you do, you'll wish you wouldn't have tried. Trust me, I tried when they took me a few hours ago. Besides, they'll most likely start drugging us to make us dependent and compliant soon after we get to wherever we are going, probably with heroin or fentanyl. Whatever hope you have, Amish girl, you might as well give up on it. There's no way out, no way home."

"I'm not giving up hope," Maria whispered fiercely, picturing Derek's face. She knew he was doing everything he could to find her and that all of CPDU would help, especially now that she might be going to the trafficking headquarters.

"No talking!" a man's loud, deep voice boomed from the front seat of the van.

The younger girl scooted over to Maria and clutched her hand, looking up at her with big blue eyes. Maria smiled ever so slightly when she saw hope glistening in them. It lifted her heavy spirit, renewing her energy.

It reminded her of her cell phone that she had tucked into her boot earlier that evening. She had been carrying her cell phone but kept it off so it wouldn't ring. And now it might just be her ticket to freedom, and for all the other women, too.

The kidnapper had searched her, but he hadn't found the phone.

CPDU could track her cell phone to her location. She just had to turn it on. She looked around to see if anyone was watching, then the girl with the black hair glared at her.

A sick feeling filled Maria's stomach. Something wasn't quite right about that young woman. Why had she been discouraging them from escaping so much? Was she just a pessimistic person, or was there more to it?

Whatever the reason, Maria had the feeling she couldn't be trusted. She'd have to wait to turn on the phone until she could do it without the young woman noticing.

***

The van stopped, and Maria felt as if her heart did, too. Maria wasn't sure if a few hours had passed or only a few minutes had slowly trickled by.

The van doors flung open, and two bulky men ordered them to get out, waving their guns. Maria looked around and tried to memorize her surroundings as best as she could. They were at what seemed to be an old abandoned warehouse. She had no idea where they were.

The men herded them into the musty building, into a large room, and locked the doors. Once the group of women dispersed, she realized there were already several other girls and women in the room. She scanned the faces for Liz and Anna.

"Maria!"

She whirled around to see the two women running toward her, then practically throwing themselves onto her. She hugged them back, and tears of gratitude flowed down her cheeks. Dirt was smeared across their faces and dresses, and there were bruises on their faces and arms.

"I'm so happy I found you. Are you hurt? What's happened?" she asked them, looking them over for more injuries, inspecting their bruises.

Anger welled up inside her against the men who had done this to them. But the bruises proved they had put up a fight.

"We are okay so far, except that Liz cut her leg while trying to get away from the men when they took her. I've been trying to take care of it, but as you can see I have no supplies," Anna said, gesturing to Liz's leg, which was bandaged with a torn off piece of clothing. "We've been in this room since we were taken. We've heard them talking about who among us will be"—she paused, her eyes lowering along with her voice—"sold first."

Liz burst into tears. "I just want to go back to the farm. I should have never gone out to the barn alone. What's going to happen to us?"

"You're a long way from the farm now," the girl with the black hair remarked coldly from a distance away, arms crossed. "I told you. There's no way out of this."

"Don't listen to her," Maria whispered. She leaned in close, so that only they could hear. "Don't say anything, but I have a cell phone hidden in my boot. CPDU is looking for us."

Liz and Anna didn't react outwardly, but Maria saw their eyes light up. She would have to turn on the phone without anyone noticing. The last thing she wanted was for one of the girls to notice and draw attention, especially the one who had discouraged them from trying to escape.

"Come on. Let's pray together," she said, and Liz and Anna followed her.

Maria moved to a corner of the room, sat down and leaned against the wall, as if praying. Liz and Anna huddled around her to help hide what she was doing.

Maria pulled her phone out of the boot that was closer to the wall and hid the phone behind her dress, then turned it on. It made some noises when it turned on, but since some of the women were talking, no one could hear it, and Maria immediately turned down the volume. She took her prayer *kapp* off and set it on top of the phone to cover it up in case she had to move quickly. Derek had once told her that as long as the phone remained on, the phone's location could be tracked.

Maria wasn't sure how much time had passed, but some time later, the door opened with a loud creak and two of the men entered. "You, there, you come with us," one of them said, and Maria's heart clenched when she realized he was pointing to her. She would have to leave the phone behind, but it didn't matter. By now Derek would have hopefully alerted CPDU to be on the lookout for her phone's location.

She stood up, and when she didn't move fast enough, one of them stomped over and pulled her out of the room.

As they led her away, she locked eyes with her two friends, hoping this wouldn't be the last time she would ever see them again.

***

"Derek. Maria's phone just turned on," Branson said on the phone. "We tracked it, and we've got a location. I'm texting it to you now. Get the team together, and I'll send a team to meet you where you are. Derek, this could be the trafficking headquarters. We might finally shut these guys down for good."

Relief and gratitude washed over Derek. *Thank you, Lord,* he prayed. "You have no idea how happy I am to hear that."

"Go get 'em."

Derek hung up, anticipation coursing through him. Ben was going to stay with Carter, and Maria's parents were on their way home. Since they were traveling by bus, it would take them more than a day to get home.

He kneeled down in front of the boy, staring into his sweet face. Derek loved this kid so much, and he loved this place. He loved the way the Amish lived, always putting family first.

"You stay here and play with Ben and your grandparents. I'm going to look for your mom, buddy."

"Promise you'll bring her home?" Carter's eyes filled with tears.

Derek threw his arms around him, the urge to protect the boy and his mother overpowering him, along with the desire to call them family.

He knew he wasn't supposed to make promises. But he wasn't supposed to fall in love with the woman he was protecting and her son, either.

"I promise I won't come back without her, kid," he said. He thanked Ben and walked out the door.

***

One of the men threw Maria down roughly onto a chair and began tying her to it. Nauseating fear overcame her when she spotted a collection of knives on the other end of the room. What were those for?

The man who had been stalking her approached her menacingly. "Your bodyguard isn't here now, is he?"

A sob welled up in her, but she swallowed it.

He pulled a gun from his belt and pointed it at her. "Now, you tell us everything you know. Trevor told us that he had told you information about our business."

So Trevor had lied to these men? Why, so they could kill her when he couldn't, since he was in jail?

"He's lying. He hates me, so I guess this is his way of taking his revenge out on me," she told the man shakily.

"Who do you think I'm going to believe? The one man who made me more money than any of my other pimps or you? A silly Amish woman dating a sad widower?"

"We aren't dating." How did he know about Derek's late wife?

"Oh, I've seen the looks you two give each other. I saw it that first night he came to your house. I could tell right away he had feelings for you, which made this whole thing even better for me," he spat, his rancid breath floating over her. Realization and disgust filled her, and she turned her face away. "You have three seconds to start talking."

"I don't know anything!" she screamed, fear pounding through her with every heartbeat.

"Three, two—"

"Trevor never told me any information!"

Was this how she would die? All because of Trevor's lie? She pictured Carter, her parents, and Derek. *Lord, please let me see them again.*

"Bring in her friend," the stalker spat. "Maybe then she'll talk."

***

After the new team that Branson sent met up with Derek's team, they set out for Maria's location. They approached the building where Maria was being held, got out of their vehicles, and traveled on foot. They stopped behind a building across the street.

From this distance, they could see three men guarding the outside of the building, but there were possibly more. They looked like regular men just standing around, but Derek was sure they were all armed and trained on how to use their weapons well.

The team leader gave the signal, then they used AR15 rifles with silencers to take out the guards.

The team split up. Some of them crept around one side of the building, and some went around the other. Derek's group headed for the door of the building while the other groups searched for more guards.

Another guard came barreling around the corner, gun raised, but Derek immediately fired. The muffled pop of the gun filled the air as the man went down.

The rest of Derek's team came around the corner. After confirming all the guards had been taken out, they prepared to enter the building.

***

Inside, one of the other men dragged a wriggling Anna into the room where Maria was being held, her wide eyes filled with fear above tear-streaked cheeks. He held her with a knife at her throat.

"Or, instead of killing you, we'll just kill her," the stalker seethed. "Or just throw her in the van outside and transport her to where she could be bought by one of my many eager buyers."

A sick shiver snaked down Maria's spine.

"Leave her alone! Please believe me. I'm Amish. The Amish don't lie," she begged.

"Everyone lies, missy. Ready to talk now, Maria?"

The way he said her name made her heart feel as though it would burst with sickening terror.

He cocked his gun. Anna cried out for him to let her live. Maria's head spun with fear, guilt, and hopelessness. Her friend was about to die, and there was nothing she could do. "Three, two, one—"

"Sebastian, wait!" The girl with the black hair strode in and crossed her arms. "I heard them talking about escaping. I found this under her bonnet thing in the corner." The girl held up Maria's smashed cell phone. "By now the police have probably already traced the phone. We don't have time for any more questions or to kill anyone. We've got to go, boss. Right now. They could be here any second."

So the girl was working for the traffickers after all. *Good thing I didn't take my phone out in front of her,* Maria thought.

Sebastian lowered his gun and let out an exasperated growl. Before she could react, his fist knocked Maria in the face. Pain erupted in her skull.

"Why didn't any of you search her, you idiots?"

"But... But one of the guys did search her."

"Apparently not well enough! Amateurs," Sebastian snapped, throwing his hands in the air. "What other secrets do you have up your sleeve, missy? Or should I say, in your boot?" He brought his face close to hers, and she wanted to crawl under her chair, but she couldn't move from where she sat. He straightened, to her relief. "You're right, Alexis," he said to the girl who had been spying for them. "We don't have time for this. Load up all the girls into the vans. We have to get out of here right now. I said now!"

All the doors to the building burst open, and dozens of CPDU officers and agents stormed the warehouse, shouting commands and aiming their weapons on the kidnappers. The man holding Anna whirled around in surprise, cutting Anna's face.

"You're surrounded! Lay down your guns or we'll shoot!" Derek ordered, and Maria's heart swelled with love for him. When this was all over, she would tell him the truth. She loved him, and she would somehow figure out a way for them to be together.

Most of the kidnappers complied, slowly putting down their guns. All except the man who had stalked her and held her son and friend at gunpoint.

229

"Sebastian, we have no choice! Drop your gun!" Alexis told him, holding her hands up.

Sebastian continued to aim his gun on Maria. Her heart fell into her stomach.

"Derek," she whispered, staring at him in desperation. Derek's eyes filled with anger and determination.

Derek fired and hit Sebastian in the torso. From the floor, Sebastian fired his gun at Derek. Maria screamed as Derek clutched his bleeding leg and the CPDU agents spread out across the building.

Sebastian wouldn't go down without a fight and shot at one of the agents, but he was immediately surrounded by three agents and handcuffed.

"I'll make you pay again, Turner," Sebastian said eerily as they dragged him out of the building to an ambulance. "And you, Amish lady, you better keep watching your back."

Maria shuddered, but her thoughts of Sebastian's threats were quickly overwhelmed by worry for Derek. Officers arrested all of the kidnappers and Alexis as Anna ran to Maria and freed her from the chair.

Anna was saying something, but Maria was only focusing on Derek. Everything felt like it was happening in slow motion. The voices around her sounded like gibberish as she dropped to the floor beside Derek. Paramedics pushed her back, then carried him away to another ambulance.

Anna wrapped Maria in a hug, and Maria realized they were both sobbing. She let Anna support her weight, then they slowly dropped to the floor, crying on each other, until one of the CPDU agents led them outside. Maria's tears turned to tears of joy as the other kidnapped girls and women walked out of the warehouse toward freedom. Soon they would be reunited with their families.

Thank you, Lord, for answering my prayer. Thank you for using me to help rescue them, she prayed. *Please take care of Derek and heal him quickly.*

CHAPTER SEVENTEEN

"If it wasn't for you, we wouldn't have found the trafficking ring headquarters. We arrested Sebastian Creed, the man who killed Natalia. He survived his gunshot wound, so we are able to question him," Branson told Maria in a somber voice as he stood in Derek's hospital room with the two of them and Ben. "I speak for all of CPDU when I say thank you."

Ben said, "It was all about revenge for Sebastian. He stalked you only to get back at Derek for arresting his brother Thomas and putting him in jail for life. He enlisted help from several other gang members to help him. We were outnumbered the entire time."

"Well, I'm so happy all of those girls and women are safe at home with their families. Some were lured into it by being told they would be models; some were picked up at the Maine Mall by the young pimps," Maria said.

"Traffickers also put out several kinds of fake job offers to lure in women," Ben said with disgust.

"Thank God they weren't transported before CPDU got there," Maria said, sitting by Derek's bedside. She hadn't left since he had arrived at the hospital, and she had waited while he was in surgery.

But so many doctors, nurses, and visitors had been in and out that they had barely had a moment alone.

"Yes. The trafficking ring has finally been shut down. It's a drop in the bucket of human trafficking, but we've been after that ring for over four years. Maine is a safer place now. It's good to know justice has been served for those women. As for the other girls and women who have already been sold through that ring, CPDU is working to find them using information from the kidnappers that they arrested at the warehouse. We've offered them deals in exchange for information. Some of them are cooperating." Branson smiled. "It feels good knowing that they won't be able to kidnap anyone else."

"Definitely. Now my hometown is back to normal. Safe and sound." Maria smiled at Derek, and he grinned back at her weakly. "What about the girl who was helping them. Alexis, was it?"

"She was kidnapped like the rest of them and was forced to act as their spy, telling Sebastian when the girls would plan to escape. They told her they would kill her if she didn't spy on the girls. Poor thing." Branson sighed heavily, shaking his head.

"She was just as afraid as the rest of the women," Ben added.

"Will she go to prison?" Maria asked.

"CPDU is working on getting her a deal. No jail time in exchange for information she has on more sex trafficking rings and where more girls are being kept. So far, she has been very helpful," Branson explained.

"That's excellent news. Thanks for giving us an update," Derek said, shifting in his hospital bed.

"No problem. Well, we will leave you two alone. Feel better, Turner," Branson said with a wry smile, putting his police hat back on and walking out the door.

"Thank you, Captain Branson. And thank you, Ben, for everything," Derek said.

"Glad you're safe now, ma'am," Ben said to Maria with a smile, and they walked out.

"Yes, thanks to both of you." Derek turned to her after the two men left, smiling again. "Thanks for sticking around with me and keeping me company."

"Of course. There's nowhere else I'd rather be." She reached forward and warmly grasped his hand, and he squeezed hers. "I know it will take you a while to recover from your surgery. I will stick around for that too, even after that. I want to stay by your side for a long time, Derek."

"I was hoping you'd say that. You know, the reason Sebastian stalked and attacked you was only to get back at me. He could tell I had—have—feelings for you. This is what I meant when I said I don't want to put people I care about in danger because of my job."

"He did say that he could tell that very first night he was in the woods at my house and you came over," Maria said, remembering when Sebastian had strapped her to the chair in the warehouse.

"He must have seen the way I looked at you." Derek gazed into Maria's eyes. "It was probably obvious that I was fascinated with you right from the start. And it almost got you killed."

"This is not your fault, Derek. That man is a sociopath."

"There is something you should know. I wanted to tell you sooner, but we haven't had any time to ourselves. I told Branson when he got here and you were down in the cafeteria," Derek said, his tone serious. His dark eyes stared at her intently. "It's not good news."

She sat up straighter. "What is it?"

"The bullet ruined my shin bone. Surgery helped, but they told me I won't be able to walk without a limp again, and I won't be able to run like I used to. I'll have chronic leg pain, and I'll need physical therapy. The point is, I won't be able to work at CPDU anymore." When he said the last sentence, he looked away from her and stared out the window. His voice dropped to a whisper. "The man who killed my wife also stole my career and damaged my leg. I don't understand how the Amish can just forgive and forget. I wish I could."

"It's hard, but we do it with God's help," Maria said, her chest constricting with sympathy for Derek.

He was right; Sebastian had taken so much from him, but it would be so freeing for Derek if he could forgive the man.

"Anyway, I wanted to tell you that before you said anything else to me. You know, in case it changed things. I know the Amish are hard workers, and I can't do as much as I used to, but I will find something that I can do well. I will do my best." Derek looked back at her and squeezed her hand. "You deserve a man who can provide for you."

She shook her head at the thought of him thinking he was not worthy of her. "You sound like you're thinking about joining the Amish," she said slowly. "Are you?"

"Actually, yes. I have no family, but your entire community is one big family. I love your church, how everyone puts their neighbor before themselves, and how it is all one big unit. I love the slow-paced and simple life style without the worldly clutter and chaos. I want to be a part of that more than anything. I want my faith back."

"But you would have to give up everything you know. Your apartment, your car…"

He shrugged. "Those are just things. I already have lost two of the things in life that I valued the most. I don't want to lose you, too, Maria. I'd do anything to be with you." He reached up and touched her face tenderly, and she closed her eyes, leaning closer to him. "And I have a confession to make," he added.

She opened her eyes and gave him a suspicious and playful look. "What?"

"I looked through your sketchbook right after you were kidnapped, and I saw the picture you drew of me and the one of us together. That's when I realized that maybe there is a slight, teeny-tiny chance that you feel the same way about me as I feel about you." He looked up at her expectantly, unasked questions filling his eyes.

Her face broke out into a grin, and warmth filled her. "I know I tried to push you away, but I never imagined you would ever even consider joining the Amish. I didn't think there was any chance for us. I thought you would be leaving after you caught the criminal. I thought I'd never see you again after this was over."

"You honestly thought after all of that, that I would leave and never think of you again? After everything we went through, how close we became?"

"I didn't know what kind of man you were. Or if it was just a summer fling for you. I don't trust very easily."

He shifted as much as he could in the bed so that he could grasp her hand with both of his own. "Maria, it was never a summer fling for me. I loved you since the moment I first saw you shooting down those bank robbers and saving that little girl's life. I could tell instantly what kind of woman you are, the kind who always put others before herself. I never thought I would love anyone else after my wife died, but I have fallen hopelessly, undeniably, deeply in love with you, Maria Mast."

She stood up and leaned over his hospital bed, bringing her face down to his. "I love you too, Derek Turner." She brought her lips to his and kissed him, feeling as if her soul was smiling. The kiss was everything she had imagined it would be: passionate, tender, and perfect.

She pulled away and quipped, "I always thought you looked good in Amish clothes."

"So that's why you were staring at me when I first put them on and came downstairs that day. I thought it was because you thought I looked silly."

"No. Of course not. I thought you looked great, but it was strange to see my late husband's clothes on you. I didn't know what to think of it. I guess I better get used to it. I can make you some clothes of your own, of course."

Derek let out a dramatic sigh of relief. "Oh, good. Because if you think my cooking is bad, just wait until you see my sewing."

***

Selling his guns had been easier than Derek expected, though it felt odd to no longer have a weapon strapped to his side. As he cleaned out his apartment, getting rid of things was freeing.

He picked up his framed photos of him and Natalia, and mixed emotions filled him.

It had been four years since he had lost his wife, and it was time to let go of the past. Even though a part of her would always be with him, he loved Maria now.

Even though the Amish didn't allow photographs of themselves, he would be allowed to have photos of outsiders like his friends and family. However, he wanted to let everything go from his past. He took the photos out of the frames and lit them with a match, watching them slowly burn.

He expected to be filled with sorrow and regret, but peace settled over his soul. He wanted to cut all ties to his former life so he could fully immerse himself into his new home and way of life.

"Goodbye, Natalia," he murmured. He would never forget her, but he had a new life waiting for him now.

Now that his leg was doing better, he packed up his car with his few belongings and drove to Unity. The Welcome to Unity sign was indeed a welcoming sight. This was home now.

He moved in with Simon Hodges and sold his car. He was dropped off at the Masts' farm.

When she saw him exit the taxi, Maria ran to him. "You're here! For good!" She ran into his open arms, holding him close. He breathed in her clean linen scent, now mingled with the smells of the barn from her morning chores.

"Yes, Maria. I'm not going anywhere," he said into her prayer *kapp.*

"Was it hard to get rid of most of your things?" she asked, pulling away to face him.

"Not as hard as I thought." He remembered the photos he had burned, but as he looked into Maria's face, his past before her seemed like a distant memory. "I am gaining so much more than I lost."

CHAPTER EIGHTEEN

Mary smiled at Derek. "I am so glad to see you!" she exclaimed. "I can't believe we weren't here for everything that happened."

"To be honest, I'm glad you weren't there. You know you would have been a worrying wreck." Maria laughed.

"You're right. Anyway, I'm so glad we're safe now."

"I can't imagine how terrifying it all was," Gideon added, shaking his head slowly.

"Mom was so brave. She helped catch all those bad men!" Carter cried, a proud grin on his boyish face.

"So you've told us," Mary said.

Derek messed up his hair playfully. "That's right. Your mom is a hero."

Maria blushed. "Oh, stop it. All I did was turn on my phone."

"If that were me, I would have never thought to do that. Well, I wouldn't have a cell phone to begin with." Mary chuckled.

"We are just happy that we are all safe now. We are so sorry to hear about your leg, Derek," Gideon said sympathetically, gesturing toward Derek's cast. "Speaking of which, Maria tells me you need a new job. It just so happens that I am looking to fill a position in my cabinet making shop, and you would certainly be able to do it in your physical condition. What do you say?"

"Actually, yes. That sounds perfect. My father and I used to build things for fun when I was younger. I always enjoyed it." Derek grinned, the gratitude on his face obvious. "I would be happy to apply. Thank you so much."

"The job is yours. I'd be happy to have you join our company."

Derek smiled at Maria, excitement radiating from him. He had been so worried about finding a job in the Amish community, and the Lord had already answered his prayer. "Simon was kind enough to rent a room out to me in his house. Everything is falling into place."

There was a knock on the door. Maria walked to the entryway to see Anna standing there. A bandage covered a good portion of her face, protecting the cut she had received at the warehouse. She pulled open the door. "Anna, how good to see you. Come in. How is your cut?"

"It's getting better, but the doctor said it will probably leave a scar." Anna's expression was somber, and she heaved a sigh. "But that's not what I came to tell you. I have come to say goodbye, Maria. I'm leaving. For good."

"Leaving?" Maria gasped.

"I'm leaving the Amish. I'm going to become a nurse," Anna told her, finality in her tone. "I believe it is my calling. After taking care of Liz's leg when we were kidnapped and treating some of the other women's injuries, I have realized there is so much more I could do outside of the Amish." Determination and anticipation shone in her eyes.

"This is what you really want? What about Simon?" Mary asked.

Everyone else had meandered into the entryway by now, listening to the conversation intently.

"I just broke up with him. I like Simon, but I don't love him. I just can't picture spending the rest of my life with him. It's not fair to him. Actually, I'm really interested in Ben. We exchanged numbers and I'm going on a date with him later this week. He's so nice."

"Wow! Really? I'm happy for you. He is a nice guy. If this is what you want, then God be with you," Maria said softly, wrapping her friend in a tight hug. "I will miss you."

As their friends left, Derek and Maria remained by the door, watching them leave.

"I've been friends with her my whole life," Maria choked out, a tear escaping down her cheek. "I can't believe she is leaving, especially since I just got to see her again after so long." She looked up at Derek with a smile. "And I can't believe you're staying."

He wrapped his arm around her shoulders lovingly. "Things change. People change. If this is what she really wants, then it's for the best. She could help a lot of people."

"I know. Ben and Anna are going on a date."

"I know. He told me all about it."

"You knew? I hope it all works out for her. I know it's selfish of me to wish she would stay. It just won't be the same without her."

Derek squeezed her shoulder. "She has all kinds of adventures waiting for her."

Maria heaved a sigh. "You're right. I should be happy for her. She's so brave to go out into the world alone."

"You're brave, too, Maria," Derek whispered into her ear, grinning at her.

"Thank you."

"Come play Dutch Blitz, you two!" Carter called from the kitchen, and the couple went into the kitchen to join the rest of the family.

**

Finally, Maria could live her life without Derek following her around constantly. Not that she had minded. Now, sometimes she missed him always being with her.

But not this morning. She couldn't sleep, so she woke up even earlier than usual to draw in her sketchbook. Then she would make a big breakfast for everyone.

Maria added some shading to the side of their barn in her sketchbook and drew the rising sun coming up over the tree line. She looked up to see the real sunrise out her window, which cast a golden light over the fields.

It was time to do her chores in the barn now. She reluctantly shut her sketchbook and shoved her freshly-sharpened pencil in her apron pocket, promising herself she'd finish the drawing that night and give it to Derek.

She breathed in the fragrant morning air, even if it did smell of manure, as she walked outside. Maria had freedom to go where she wanted, when she wanted, even if it was only within the community. It felt wonderful.

She poked around for eggs in the chicken coop, skirting around the feistiest chicken, who squawked at Maria's intrusion, feathers ruffled in annoyance.

"I'm almost done, Gertrude. Just hold on a second." Maria snatched up a few more eggs out of their wooden compartments that Gideon had built and darted out of the coop, holding on tightly to her basket full of eggs.

While she was at it, she went into the barn to feed the rest of the animals to save her parents some work. She relished the tasks, reminding her of how good it was to be home. The one word she could think of to describe her life at this point in time was *perfect*. Everyone she loved was in one place, safe, and Derek was here to stay.

Even though no one was around, she smiled. How long would it be before they were married with a house of their own? Some people desired wealth or elaborate homes, but a simple farmhouse full of kids and a good husband who truly loved her was all Maria wanted out of life.

As she finished, she thought of the breakfast she would make of French toast and sausage for her family and Derek. She held on carefully to the basket of eggs, and looked up to see a figure standing in the doorway.

What was a police officer doing here so early in the morning?

No, that was no police officer.

It was Trevor. He was wearing some type of security guard uniform, staring at her maliciously, hatred written on his face. Dread and horror seeped into her bones, and she stiffened as a dozen questions arose within her. How had he gotten out of jail? Where could she go? How could she escape from him?

Was he here to finally kill her, as he always said he would?

"You look hot in Amish clothes. You should have told me about your Amish past." He sneered as he looked her over, slowly stepping closer. Maria choked back the bile rising in her throat.

He continued, "You went and got me arrested. Again. Do you know how many years I got? That's why I escaped. If you only knew the stuff that already happened to me in jail… This time, you're really going to pay."

The hate in his eyes made her feet fly. She wouldn't be able to get past him through the door, so not knowing what else to do, she ran to the other end of the barn, dropping her basket of eggs.

She was trapped. Since there was only one door, Maria had no idea how she would get out, but she had to try.

Maria scrambled past pigpens and horse stalls, darting around bales of hay, desperation fueling her. She ran into one of the empty stalls and gently shut it, then crouched in the corner, her heart pounding so hard she wondered if he could hear it.

What, did she think he would give up looking for her and leave? He would eventually find her. A sick feeling churned in her stomach, knowing it would be only a matter of minutes. In the other corner of the barn there was a rake. Carter must have left it in there after helping muck the stalls. She crawled over to it, gripped it tightly, and waited. When he came, she'd be ready.

Yes, she'd rejoined the Amish, and she loved the Amish way of life and agreed with most of its rules, but she realized she didn't agree with their views on pacifism at all.

Maria wouldn't just let Trevor take her or hurt her. She'd fight him with everything she had.

His footsteps echoed throughout the barn. "Where are you hiding, Maria? Do you really think I won't find you?" he taunted. "Come on out. This is pointless."

Maria gripped the rake tighter, ready to fight. Trevor appeared in the doorway of the stall, flinging open the door. She swung the rake at his head, but he ducked swiftly and leapt at her, knocking her to the hay-covered floor. He grappled it out of her hands, and despair set in when she realized how much stronger than her he really was.

She had thought that she was safe since the stalker had been arrested. She realized she should have continued to carry her cell phone and pepper spray.

Maybe she should have continued to secretly carry her gun, even though it would risk her getting shunned.

Getting shunned again would be better than getting killed.

Trevor pinned her hands down. "You always did put up a good fight. That's admirable. But it never got you anywhere." He pulled some rope out of his pocket along with a knife. He held it to her throat, and she remembered the way Anna had looked in the same situation. She was sure her eyes looked as wide as hers had, fear shining in them.

"If you cooperate, I won't hurt you. I won't hurt your son or new boyfriend, either. Okay? Now hold still."

Feeling the cold steel against her neck paralyzed her, and she let him tie her hands.

She had no choice. When Trevor threatened her and those she loved, she didn't think for a second that he was bluffing.

CHAPTER NINETEEN

Sunlight woke Derek. He stretched, then rolled over to check his phone in his tiny bedroom in Simon's house. When it wasn't on his nightstand, he realized he had left it in the basement to charge. He also realized he was still wearing his clothes from the day before. He had meant to get the phone before he went to bed, but he must have fallen asleep first.

A bad feeling settled deep in his gut. Something was wrong. He could feel it. He took the steps to the basement two at a time, snatching the phone up and swiping the screen. He had several recent missed calls and texts from Branson and Martin, all screaming one thing: Trevor had escaped jail. Maria was in danger. Good thing he still had his phone. Once he joined the church, he wouldn't use a phone anymore, but for now he still had it.

Blue and red lights flashed in the basement windows. Derek grabbed his crutches and went outside.

"You're a hard guy to get a hold of, Turner! I've been calling you over and over. What happened? You joined the Amish and fell off the face of the planet?" Officer Martin called, exiting his car. "We just found out that Trevor escaped jail less than an hour ago. He bribed a correctional officer to give him a uniform and help him escape after he faked a seizure and they were transporting him to the hospital. We don't quite know yet how long he has been loose. Where is Maria?"

"Hopefully at home," Derek murmured, urgency pounding through him as he hobbled as quickly as he could to the Masts' farmhouse. He burst through their front door, now left unlocked because they thought they were safe since the stalker was gone. "Maria?" he called throughout the house.

"Derek? What's wrong?" Mary opened her bedroom door. Though she was dressed in her blue frock and head covering, sleep lingered in her eyes as if she had just woken up. Gideon appeared next to her.

"Trevor escaped jail."

He climbed the stairs, wishing he could move faster. Frustration at his new disability burned within him. He barged into her bedroom, which was empty, but the bed was made. The colorful quilt stretched over the bed without one wrinkle. She had not been taken from her bedroom.

"I heard her get up early this morning and go out to the barn. It was just before dawn. We got up shortly after. It was only a few minutes ago," Mary explained as she followed Derek back down the stairs.

"Every minute is crucial." Derek slammed open the front door and hurried to the barn.

Maria's parents shot ahead of him, along with Martin, and Mary let out a gasp when they reached the barn doorway.

Her hands covered her mouth when they saw the basket of broken eggs on the ground. "What has happened to our daughter?" Tears spilled from her eyes, and Gideon wrapped his arms around his wife, one of the few outward displays of affection Derek had witnessed from any of the Amish couples.

"He took her," Derek told them, his throat tightening.

Mary cried out in despair as Derek stomped out into the yard, studying the driveway, using his crutch to poke at the dirt, where he spotted two sets of footprints in the dirt. He followed their tracks into the woods, where tire tracks led to the lane and dug into the gravel. From the looks of the smaller set, she had put up a fight. "He was definitely here."

"Let's go, Turner." Martin opened the door of his car and got in.

As dread knotted his stomach and indignation burned against the man who took the woman he loved, he turned to face Mary and Gideon. "I will find her. I have to find her." He looked heavenward before getting into Martin's car. "God, help me find her."

***

"Let's go." Trevor pulled Maria roughly to her feet and dragged her outside.

Most of the community was still sleeping or doing early morning chores. No one else was in sight. Trevor must have been watching her, waiting to get her alone.

He led her to a gray car that was hidden in the woods, and she made one last ditch effort to wrench herself away from his grip, but he only clutched her tighter. He brought the knife up to her throat.

One sentence from a self-defense class rang through Maria's mind: *Do anything you can do avoid getting in the car with a kidnapper.*

She wracked her brain for ideas on how she could escape. If only she had a weapon on her...

Then she remembered the sharp pencil in her apron pocket. The question was, how could she get it in her hand without him noticing?

She pretended to trip, bending over in order to try to snatch the pencil out of her pocket. Her fingers brushed it, but she didn't have enough time to grab it before he pulled her upright.

"Watch where you're going," he said with a snarl. "No funny business. I'm warning you."

She stilled, pretending to give in to his power, knowing he wouldn't hesitate before slicing her throat. As they reached the car, she wondered where his usual white truck was, but she said nothing. For all she knew, this was stolen. He opened the trunk, and her stomach sank.

Derek's face filled her mind. He would be sick with worry and guilt when he found out she had been taken. He hadn't been there to protect her, yet he had been right next door. If she was killed, she wasn't sure what he would do.

Hopefully, it wouldn't come to that.

A police car sped toward them and Trevor fired, bullets pounding on the front of the car. Maria had no idea if the glass was bulletproof.

It was the distraction she needed. She reached down with her bound hands and grabbed the pencil out of her apron pocket, gripping it tightly in her fist.

Derek leaned out the passenger side as the car swung around and stopped. "Let her go!"

"No! Make one wrong move and I'll shoot her!" Trevor pressed the knife to her throat, and Maria stared at Derek's face, focusing on him.

She winked at him, and he nodded slightly in response, just like he had at the bank, though he looked a little confused.

As Trevor yelled obscenities at them, she jammed the pencil as hard as she could into Trevor's thigh. When he backed away from her and dropped his knife, finally releasing her as he fell to the ground in agony, Martin jumped out of the car and ran straight for Trevor. Derek couldn't travel very fast, so Maria bolted toward him and fell into his open arms.

She was aware of everything about him: his clean scent, his muscular arms holding her tight, his soft hair and strong back. As she let him hold her and she buried her face into his shirt, she listened to the clicking of handcuffs. Martin read Trevor his rights and pushed him into the police car.

She was safe for real this time. Trevor was going back to prison, and this time it would be for good.

Maria had to decide what she would do about her views on self-defense that completely went against Amish rules. Now that she'd lived outside the community and had defended herself several times, she couldn't just pretend like she was fine with acting like self-defense was wrong.

Maria looked up at Derek, who had given up his entire way of life and sold all his weapons to live among the Amish. Deep down, did he feel the same way about pacifism as she did? Or was he completely in agreement with the ways of the community?

Would they conform their belief on the subject to align with Amish rules, or would they keep that part of their lives a secret?

Maria wasn't sure yet, but she knew they would figure it out together.

***

Several months later…

As Derek waited for Sebastian to meet him in jail, his heart clenched, a mixture of emotions swirling within him. He knew he had to do this if he was going to give his heart to God and join the Amish. Forgiveness was one of the most important things in their lives, and there was no way he could call himself a true Amish man or Christian if he continued to hold a grudge against the man who had killed his wife.

Maria wasn't allowed to see Sebastian, since that would constitute a felony violation for Sebastian and result in serious problems for prosecution of the case. Even Derek had to jump through several hoops just to be here, and it had taken a while, but here he was.

A guard stood stiffly nearby as Derek fidgeted in his chair, staring at the chair across from him on the other side of the glass wall.

Seeing Sebastian once again would exhume horrific memories of his wife's death and Maria's abduction, but he would have to endure it in order to talk to his wife's killer. This man had a long list of charges against him, his wife being only one of several kills that this man had made.

And his leg being only one of the ways Sebastian left a trail of hurt behind him everywhere he went. Derek instinctively put his hand over the healed bullet wound, wincing at the memory of the bullet ripping through it.

But it had been a small price to pay for rescuing Maria and the other girls and shutting down the ring. It had been completely worth it.

The sound of footsteps and clinking metal echoed as another guard brought in a handcuffed Sebastian. Coldness and hate glinted in his steely eyes as he eased into the chair across from Derek and picked up the phone that they would use to communicate on his side of the glass.

"Why are you here, Turner?" the trafficker said into the phone, smirking. "I don't know why you would ever want to see me, which made this all the more interesting. So I cleared my busy schedule for the day. If I had known you were coming today, I would have ironed my nicer orange jumpsuit. How's that leg doing?"

"I have something I want to talk to you about."

"What's with the getup?" Sebastian's eyes looked Derek up and down, eyeing his linen shirt, suspenders and dark pants. "What, did you quit CPDU and join the Amish or something?"

"Actually, yes."

Sebastian let out a long, haggard laugh that lacked mirth, cackling at the end, the effects of long-term smoking taking its toll on his voice. "Well, I figured you would be useless to CPDU after that bullet wounded you. I really didn't expect that you'd join the Amish. Serves you right for putting my brother in prison for life, and now me."

A flash of anger tore through Derek, but he tamped it down. So Sebastian's shot had been intentional. He could have killed him, but instead the man chose to prevent him from doing his job. It was a daily reminder of Sebastian's revenge and that he was indeed useless to CPDU. But it didn't matter. All that mattered was that he still had Maria and that the other girls were safe.

"Well, I did join. Which is why I am here." Derek leaned forward, resting his elbows on the table, looking right into Sebastian's eyes. The image of Natalia's corpse and the warehouse full of terrified girls filled his mind, but he briefly closed his eyes to will them away. The pain would linger, but that would fade with time. "The Amish always forgive those who hurt them, no matter what. I know I need to forgive you, so that is why I am here. To tell you I forgive you."

"But I killed your late wife, you crazy man. I shot you in the leg. I kidnapped your girlfriend. I was going to sell her and all those other girls to the highest bidder. And you want to forgive me?" Sebastian asked incredulously.

"Yes. It's what Jesus would do, and it is what the Bible tells me I should do," Derek explained simply.

Sebastian let out another humorless laugh, letting his head rest on the table. "You've got to be kidding me."

"Nope."

"Wow. You're a piece of work, you know that, Turner?"

An incredible burden lifted off Derek's shoulders, and he smiled compassionately at the criminal. This man needed Jesus desperately. Derek put a Bible and devotional book on the table. "I brought these for you. My life has been changed by God, and I hope one day you might understand what that is like."

Sebastian spat on the floor, and the guard yelled at him. Sebastian ignored him, staring Derek down. "God? Jesus? Seriously, man. Get a grip. I kidnapped and sold women for a living. If there is a God, He must hate my guts."

"There is a God, and He loves you. And you need His forgiveness," Derek told him, standing. "I'll be back to see you. So you better iron that nicer orange jumpsuit after all." Derek put the phone back.

Leaving Sebastian speechless for once in his life, Derek walked to the door, then stopped when he realized the gray-haired guard who had been standing nearby had tears in his eyes.

"In all my years working here, I have never witnessed anything like that before," the man choked out, blinking a tear away and standing up straighter. "That takes guts, sir."

"No. It takes God."

CHAPTER TWENTY

Derek stepped out of the driver's car and paid him, since he had sold his own car. He walked to the Masts' farm, leaning on his cane. He hadn't felt this free or joyful in so long. Finally, his heart was at peace. The painful memories didn't seem as painful as they had been, and it was clear that he could move on now.

He knocked on the Masts' door and Mary answered. "Hello, Derek. How are you today?"

He could hear the sound of dishes being washed in the background. They had probably just finished eating dinner. "Very good, thank you. I'd like to take a walk with Maria if she is here."

"Oh, yes. Maria!"

Maria appeared, wiping her hands with a damp towel. He loved to watch the way her face brightened when she saw him, and it warmed his heart. Mary made herself scarce, and Derek tugged on Maria's hand.

"Where are we going?"

"For a walk. Come on."

She tossed her towel aside and followed him down the porch stairs and to the lane.

"I went to see Sebastian."

"You did? Why?" Maria asked, the setting sun casting honey colored light on her face. He hadn't been able to speak of the matter to anyone, not even Maria. He wasn't sure if it had been because it was hard to talk about or that he had been afraid he was not going to be able to forgive Sebastian, despite his best intentions.

"I had to forgive him."

Maria stopped and gently took hold of his arm, looking up at him as he stopped too. "Oh, Derek. That must have been so hard. I know how much pain that man has caused you."

"Actually, it wasn't as hard as I thought it was going to be." Derek said as they continued walking. "I told him I was joining the Amish and that God wanted me to forgive him, so I did. And I gave him a Bible and a devotional. He didn't seem interested and he laughed at me, calling me crazy. But who knows. God can use even the worst of criminals and change their hearts. Now a burden has been lifted from me."

"Absolutely. I am so happy for you." She looped her arm through his and squeezed it. "God might work a miracle in his heart. We must pray for him."

"Definitely. I will be returning to see him. To check on him."

"That is wonderful news." She looked up again, admiration shining in her eyes. "You are an amazing man, Derek Turner. You only just decided to join the Amish—you haven't even been baptized into the church yet—and you have more forgiveness in your heart than anyone I know."

"It was all because of God."

Maria smiled a knowing smile, admiring the changing trees around them with leaves the color of fire. "All of this was. Everything that has happened."

As they approached the old barn, Derek's heart pounded, making him feel as if his throat had plummeted into his stomach. "Maria, there is something I must ask you."

She turned to him, listening.

He knew that the Amish did not wear engagement or wedding rings, but he did not know much about how Amish men proposed.

"I would kneel, but my leg wouldn't allow it," Derek said softly, taking Maria's hands in his own. He felt his throat constricting, as if his words would not come out. She stared at him, her face growing pale, waiting expectantly. "We have been through so much together these past several months. And you know I have fallen deeply, wildly in love with you. When you were taken and I thought I'd never see you again, I just couldn't bear the thought. Now that you are safe, I don't want to waste any more time. You and Carter have given me some of the happiest times of my life. And I want those moments to continue forever. Maria, will you marry me?"

Tears glistened in Maria's eyes, and she threw her arms around him. "Yes, yes! I will marry you. I love you."

Joy, elation and excitement filled him, and his own eyes stung with tears. He held Maria close, breathing in her sweet scent. "I love you, too."

CHAPTER TWENTY-ONE

No wedding bells chimed on Maria's wedding day, and no organ played. There were no flowers or bridesmaids, and there was no white dress. Just a simple blue frock and the small church containing most of the people with whom she had grown up.

It was a sunny November day, and it had been over a year since Derek joined her Amish community. He had been warmly accepted and was enjoying his job at Gideon's cabinet shop. His leg had healed well, and his limp wasn't very obvious, but he would never be able to run again.

In the bathroom, Mary smoothed out invisible wrinkles in Maria's dress. "I know we are not supposed to compliment one another's outward appearances, but you look beautiful, my darling." She sighed, pulling Maria into her arms. "And I couldn't have picked out a better man for you if I tried."

Maria hugged her mother tightly, tears stinging her eyes as she adjusted her white head covering. "Thank you. I cannot tell you how happy I am."

"It's obvious. You and Derek were made for each other." Mary cleared her throat in an effort to hold back her own tears, but they spilled from her eyes anyway. She wiped them away quickly with a finger, though there was no makeup on her face that would smudge.

"Oh, no, don't cry. You're going to make me cry!"

"I'm just so happy for you two!" Mary cried. "And Carter, too. I know he's thrilled to call Derek *Daed*." Mary smiled.

"It's time to go out there," Liz said, popping her head inside the bathroom.

Maria nodded, and they made their way out into the main room of the church.

Dozens of families mingled before her, but Maria spotted Derek in the crowd immediately. He was comfortably talking with several men that he now called close friends, holding Carter's hand. Even Ben was there, who was grinning and giving Derek a friendly slap on the back.

Derek's smile was contagious, obvious excitement radiating from him. Warmth filled her from head to toe, an overwhelming happiness. Everyone who meant anything to her was here. Except Anna, Olivia and Isaac, who had been shunned. Sadness started to creep in, but she tamped it down. She knew the three of them would not want Maria to feel the least bit sad on her wedding day.

Carter ran up to her and hugged her waist. "Mommy! You look pretty. Are you happy?"

"Thank you, baby. And yes, I'm very happy. This is one of the happiest days of my life."

"I'm so glad Derek will finally be my *Daed*," Carter said, looking up at her, smiling.

"Me too."

Several of her community members greeted her. Their conversations seemed to blur together, and her cheeks began to hurt from smiling so much. Derek made his way through the large groups of people.

"Hello, my love. How are you today?" he asked, his handsome face beaming down on her. His jaw was now smooth and hairless, but once he was married, he would let his beard with no mustache grow, just like all the other married men.

"I am happier today than I have ever been in my whole life, actually." She leaned in closer and whispered under all the loud voices around her, "I can't wait to be your wife."

"And I can't wait to be your husband."

The elders asked everyone to be seated and Maria and Derek sat in the front row. Mary took Carter's hand and they sat down with Gideon.

The service began at 9am. First, they sang very slow hymns, some in English and some in Pennsylvania Dutch. Then three speakers gave messages in English and in Pennsylvania Dutch, and there was a translator for those who only spoke English. Derek understood bits and pieces of Pennsylvania Dutch, now that he was picking up the language. It actually wasn't as hard as he thought it would be to learn.

At the end of the three-hour ceremony, Maria and Derek recited simple vows. There was no kiss and no rings, but they were pronounced husband and wife.

Joy flooded Maria's soul as she looked into the eyes of her husband. Everyone went downstairs for lunch where there was a huge spread of pies, casseroles, sandwiches, salads and cookies. There was no wedding cake, but Maria was content with their simple wedding.

After what seemed like only a few minutes, the reception came to a close and the families drove away in their buggies one by one. Maria hugged her family goodbye, who would be taking care of the cleanup. Carter hugged her tightly, then Derek.

"We are all a family now, *Daed*," Carter said, positively beaming.

Derek ruffled the boy's hair and held him close once more. "Yes, Carter. We will be a family forever."

"Your parents have to go now, Carter. We will have fun while they are away, won't we?" Gideon said. "Then, you will move into the new house with them."

Maria climbed into their new buggy, and sat close to her new husband. She leaned her head against his rugged shoulder. "This day was perfect, wasn't it?"

"Absolutely. I love you, Mrs. Turner." Derek's deep voice feathered into her ear, and she smiled, looping her arm through his.

"I love you too, Mr. Turner."

Everyone said goodbye, then Derek made a clicking sound. Their horse, Rocket, stepped forward, taking their buggy down the dirt path in a rocking motion. Maria surveyed her surroundings, taking in a deep breath. *Thank you, Lord, for this wonderful life you have given me*, she prayed.

A movement caught her eye, and she saw a flash of blonde hair. Anna, Isaac and Olivia stood in a small cluster of trees, and two other women she didn't recognize stood with them. They gave Maria a small wave. So they had attended the wedding after all, even if it meant they'd had to stand outside.

Maria waved back, tenderness and love for her friends filling her. Anna was such a sweet woman. As her friend turned away and walked away with Isaac and Olivia, Maria hoped she would truly find what she was looking for.

But she wouldn't let herself worry about that now. Anna was strong and capable, and if anyone from her community would succeed in the outside world, it would be her. Maria's friends got in a car and started following Maria and Derek. Maybe the friends wanted to congratulate the happy couple away from the church.

The buggy jostled along the lane, and the horse stopped in the driveway of their new home that the community had helped them build. Though it was a large white two-story house that they planned to fill with children, it was sturdy and simple with no added frills.

However, it did have an art studio filled with sketchpads, pencils, paints and blank canvases.

"Welcome home," she announced, jumping down from the buggy.

Derek took the horse into their barn, and Maria stood outside, gazing over the fields of their home. She could see her parents' house from here, the cabinet shop, and her friends' houses. The church was hidden in the trees, but it was not far. Everything and everyone she loved was within shouting distance. She never imagined that she would end up with such a wonderful life. Or such a wonderful husband.

Derek emerged from the barn, looking handsome in his plain wedding clothes.

Maria's friends' car pulled into their driveway. Anna, Isaac, Olivia, their friend Freya, and a beautiful woman with long, black hair exited the car and walked toward them.

Clean, well-dressed and healthy looking, Maria almost didn't recognize Alexis from the warehouse, the woman who had been forced to spy on them for the kidnappers. Freya was also with them.

"That's Alexis," Maria murmured to Derek, and they met them in the driveway.

"It's so good to see you!" Olivia grinned and threw her arms around Maria. "I missed you. Your house is lovely."

"Thanks. I missed you too."

"Congrats to both of you," Isaac said.

"Congratulations, my dear friend," Anna said and wrapped Maria in a hug.

"We are so happy for you," Freya said, also giving Maria a hug.

"I hope you understand why we didn't go inside the church," Olivia said.

Maria nodded. If they had gone inside the church, no one would have been able to speak to them, since Olivia, Isaac, and Anna were shunned. In fact, if anyone found out they were speaking to each other, Maria and Derek could be shunned as well. Still, Maria couldn't turn her friends away. "Thank you for coming anyway, though you watched from a distance. And of course I understand."

"We grew up together. We couldn't miss your wedding day. And it was beautiful," Olivia said.

Anna rubbed Maria's arm with a grin. "You look beautiful. I'm allowed to compliment your looks now."

Maria blushed. "Thank you, Anna. Wow, Alexis, you look great."

"Thanks." Alexis smiled at them. "I hope we're not interrupting. We just wanted to stop in and see you today."

Freya shook Derek's hand. "Hi, I'm Freya. We know this is your wedding day, so we can come back another time, if you'd rather."

"We just figured since we were already here, we could come say high real quick," Olivia added. "Don't worry. We will keep it quick."

"We are happy to see you! I'm so glad you came by. Come on in," Maria said, and they walked into the new house, into the kitchen.

A long row of cabinets lined the light blue wall of the kitchen, a wedding gift from Gideon. The walls were mostly bare, and in the living room were a couch and a sofa. Handcrafted furniture filled the home, along with several things her mother had given her, like a wooden chest and knitted blankets and quilts. A sturdy oak table made by Gideon graced the center of the kitchen area, one of his gifts to Derek and Maria. They sat down while Maria brought cups of water.

"I just wanted to apologize to you for what I did in the warehouse. How I spied on you. I wanted to explain," Alexis began, accepting the water.

"There's no need to apologize, Alexis," Maria said softly, resting her hand on the other woman's. "Captain Branson told us those horrible men forced you to be on their side and give them information about the kidnapped girls."

"Yes, they did. I could have refused, but I was too scared." Shame shadowed her face, and she lowered her head.

"No one blames you for what you did. You were put in an impossible situation. They would have killed you, Alexis. And you have been so valuable to CPDU, giving them information they need to rescue so many survivors of human trafficking," Derek reassured her.

"Thank you for saying so. That day in the warehouse, I wasn't going to tell them about your cell phone, but I needed something to distract him so that he would not kill Anna. When Sebastian threatens something, he does it. I knew he would shoot her. So I came in and told them about the phone, thinking maybe he'd start packing everyone up to move. But I was hoping that enough time had passed for CPDU to track the phone and get there before they loaded all the girls into the vans," Alexis explained. "And I was right. CPDU got there in time. I just wanted to tell you I am sorry that I spied on you for them."

"Alexis, you saved my life. If it wasn't for your intervention, Sebastian would have probably killed me," Anna said with an appreciative smile, wrapping her arms around Alexis' shoulders.

"Thank you, Alexis. If it wasn't for your quick thinking… We owe you so much." Maria's voice cracked with emotion at the thought of how close Anna was to death. "I had no idea at the time that you were being forced to spy for them."

Alexis sighed. "All that matters is that we are all safe now and those men have been put away."

"Anna has been teaching me about God. We are getting an apartment together, though we aren't sure where yet. We're going to be roommates." Alexis grinned at her new friend. "We are even going to nursing school together."

"That's wonderful news!" Maria exclaimed. "You will both make excellent nurses. And Freya, how are things going with Adam?"

"Very well, actually. Thanks for asking."

"Do you think he's the one?" Anna asked, giggling.

271

Freya blushed. "I hope so."

"Did you two solve the case in Smyrna?" Maria asked Olivia and Isaac.

"Yes. There was a string of robberies in the Amish community in Smyrna, but the burglars have been arrested, so now we've been able to come home," Isaac explained.

"I'm so happy to see you all today. Our wedding just wouldn't have been the same if I hadn't been able to see you all."

"Well, we don't want to keep you on this joyous day," Anna said, standing.

Olivia took Maria's and Derek's hands in her own. "We pray God blesses your marriage and your life together. You'll always be like a sister to me, Maria."

Maria's eyes stung with tears at her cousin's words as everyone exchanged hugs, then the five visitors left. Maria stepped into Derek's open arms, and he held her close as they watched from a window, waving as they drove away.

"It is so wonderful that the five of them are friends now. Anna and Alexis aren't alone in their new lives," she said softly into his arm. "And Freya and I found love after everything that happened."

"They will do great things out there and so will you." He turned her around to face him. "I should have known I was going to marry you from the second you saved that little girl," he whispered into her ear, and she laughed.

"I should have known I was going to marry you the second you devoured my bacon alfredo."

He squeezed her tightly as Maria watched the car drive farther away down the lane.

She didn't know if she would ever see her friends again. She didn't even know what would happen tomorrow.

But it was all in God's hands. She trusted Him completely. He knew best.

After all, He had gotten her this far.

***

Note from the author: I hope you enjoyed this story.

The third book, *Amish Amnesia,* is now available on Amazon! I've included an excerpt at the end of this book.

I would appreciate an honest review for *Amish Under Fire* because reviews are actually very important. They help other customers know more about my books. Your opinion matters!

Thank you! Please feel free to email me at ashley@ashleyemmaauthor.com. I'd love to talk with you.

Don't forget to visit http://www.AshleyEmmaAuthor.com/to

download free Amish books!

ABOUT THE AUTHOR

Ashley Emma knew she wanted to be a novelist for as long as she can remember. She was home-schooled and was blessed with the opportunity to spend her time focusing on reading and writing. She began writing books for fun at a young age, completing her first novella at age 12 and writing her first novel at age 14, then publishing it at age 16.

She went on to write 8 more manuscripts before age 25 when she also became a multi-bestselling author.

She owns Fearless Publishing House where she helps other aspiring authors achieve their dreams of publishing their own books.

Ashley lives in Maine with her husband and children, and she plans on releasing several more books in the near future.

Visit her at ashleyemmaauthor.com or email her at: ashley@ashleyemmaauthor.com. She loves to hear from her readers!

If you enjoyed this book, would you consider leaving a review? Reviews tremendously help authors because they help other customers decide whether or not they want to buy the book or not.

Thank you!

LOOKING FOR SOMETHING NEW TO READ?

Click here to check out other books by Ashley Emma

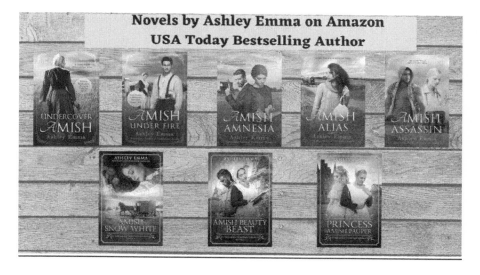

GET 4 OF ASHLEY EMMA'S AMISH EBOOKS FOR FREE

www.AshleyEmmaAuthor.com

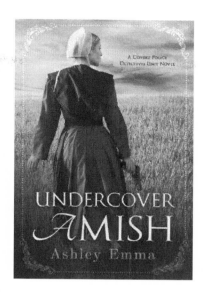

(This series can be read out of order or as standalone novels.)

Detective Olivia Mast would rather run through gunfire than return to her former Amish community in Unity, Maine, where she killed her abusive husband in self-defense.

Olivia covertly investigates a murder there while protecting the man she dated as a teen: Isaac Troyer, a potential target.

When Olivia tells Isaac she is a detective, will he be willing to break Amish rules to help her arrest the killer?

Undercover Amish was a finalist in Maine Romance Writers Strut Your Stuff Competition 2015 where it received 26 out of 27 points and has 455+ Amazon reviews!

Buy here: https://www.amazon.com/Undercover-Amish-Covert-Police-   Detectives-ebook/dp/B01L6JE49G

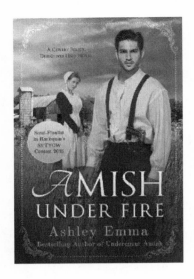

After Maria Mast's abusive ex-boyfriend is arrested for being involved in sex trafficking and modern-day slavery, she thinks that she and her son Carter can safely return to her Amish community.

But the danger has only just begun.

Someone begins stalking her, and they want blood and revenge.

Agent Derek Turner of Covert Police Detectives Unit is assigned as her bodyguard and goes with her to her Amish community in Unity, Maine.

Maria's secretive eyes, painful past, and cautious demeanor intrigue him.

As the human trafficking ring begins to target the Amish community, Derek wonders if the distraction of her will cost him his career...and Maria's life.

Buy on Amazon: http://a.co/fT6D7sM

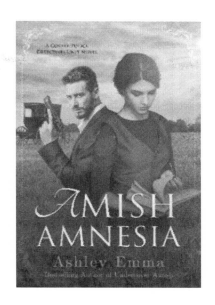

When Officer Jefferson Martin witnesses a young woman being hit by a car near his campsite, all thoughts of vacation vanish as the car speeds off.

When the malnourished, battered woman wakes up, she can't remember anything before the accident. They don't know her name, so they call her Jane.

When someone breaks into her hospital room and tries to kill her before getting away, Jefferson volunteers to protect Jane around the clock. He takes her back to their Kennebunkport beach house along with his upbeat sister Estella and his friend who served with him overseas in the Marine Corps, Ben Banks.

At first, Jane's stalker leaves strange notes, but then his attacks become bolder and more dangerous.

Buy on Amazon:

https://www.amazon.com/gp/product/B07SDSFV3

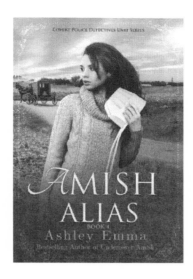

Threatened. Orphaned. On the run.

With no one else to turn to, these two terrified sisters can only hope their Amish aunt will take them in. But the quaint Amish community of Unity, Maine, is not as safe as it seems.

After Charlotte Cooper's parents die and her abusive ex-fiancé threatens her, the only way to protect her younger sister Zoe is by faking their deaths and leaving town.

The sisters' only hope of a safe haven lies with their estranged Amish aunt in Unity, Maine, where their mother grew up before she left the Amish.

Elijah Hochstettler, the family's handsome farmhand, grows closer to Charlotte as she digs up dark family secrets that her mother kept from her.

Buy on Amazon here: https://www.amazon.com/Amish-Alias-Romantic-Suspense-Detectives/dp/1734610808

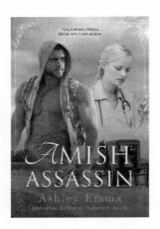

When nurse Anna Hershberger finds a man with a bullet wound who begs her to help him without taking him to the hospital, she has a choice to make.

Going against his wishes, she takes him to the hospital to help him after he passes out. She thinks she made the right decision...until an assassin storms in with a gun. Anna has no choice but to go on the run with her patient.

This handsome stranger, who says his name is Connor, insists that they can't contact the police for help because there are moles leaking information. His mission is to shut down a local sex trafficking ring targeting Anna's former Amish community in Unity, Maine, and he needs her help most of all.

Since Anna was kidnapped by sex traffickers in her Amish community, she would love nothing more than to get justice and help put the criminals behind bars.

But can she trust Connor to not get her killed? And is he really who he says he is?

Buy on Amazon:
https://www.amazon.com/gp/product/B084R9V4CN

Ever wondered what it would be like to live in an Amish community? Now you can find out in this true story with photos.

Buy on Amazon: https://www.amazon.com/Ashleys-Amish-Adventures-Outsider-community-ebook/dp/B01N5714WE

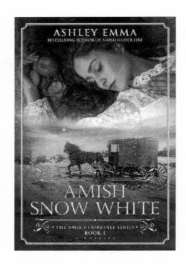

An heiress on the run.

A heartbroken Amish man, sleep-walking through life.

Can true love's kiss break the spell?

After his wife dies and he returns to his Amish community, Dominic feels numb and frozen, like he's under a spell.

When he rescues a woman from a car wreck in a snowstorm, he brings her home to his mother and six younger siblings. They care for her while she sleeps for several days, and when she wakes up in a panic, she pretends to have amnesia.

But waking up is only the beginning of Snow's story.

Buy on Amazon: https://www.amazon.com/Amish-Snow-White-Standalone-Fairytale-ebook/dp/B089NHH7D4

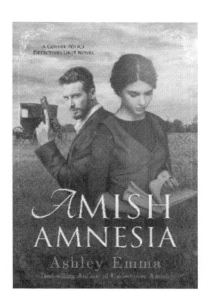

EXCERPT FROM *AMISH AMNESIA*

(This series can be read out of order or as standalone novels.)

Jefferson Martin reached his hands towards the campfire, inhaling the woodsy, smoky scent as he looked at the stars through the skeletal maze of tree branches above. After returning home from Afghanistan a few days ago, Jeff planned on spending his time off doing nothing but enjoying nature in Maine.

"Dad would have loved this," he told his sister, Estella.

"Oh yeah. He'd be making s'mores right now." Estella tossed her blonde hair over her shoulder, then smacked her forehead with a chuckle. "That's what we forgot! Stuff to make s'mores."

"Wow. I haven't had one of those since I was a kid." Jeff looked at her, grinning like the mischievous kid he used to be. "We should go to the store right now and get some, in honor of Dad."

"You mean you should go. I'll stay here and watch the fire." Estella smiled as she stoked the flames with the stick in her hand and pulled the blanket tighter around her shoulders. The night air was beginning to get chilly. "Get some coffee while you're at it, okay?"

"Okay." Jeff was already walking down the short path through the woods towards his car in the gravel parking lot near the restrooms. There was a small store a few miles down the road, and he figured it wouldn't take him more than a few minutes to drive down there and get back. He drove down the lane towards the main road, pausing at a stop sign.

He peered through the darkness at a car parked on the side of the road, curious when he heard shouting from inside the car. Suddenly a girl got out of the passenger side, and even from this far away she looked terrified and confused. She stumbled across the street, looking back at the car over her shoulder, the ragged clothing she wore hanging loosely on her thin body.

A man inside the car shouted profanities out the window at the girl. The first thing that came to Jeff's mind was domestic abuse, probably a fight between a couple. Sadly, he had seen it before. Still, his police and Marines training kicked in.

He was reaching for his door to go and offer his help anyway when the man driving veered his car out onto the street at about ten or fifteen miles an hour, as if the driver wanted to hurt her, not kill her. Jeff watched in horror as the car struck her knocked her over. She landed awkwardly on the ground with a sick thud, her body motionless on the street. The car stopped when it hit her instead of running her over, almost as if the driver was remorseful, then backed up.

Jeff slammed his foot down on the gas and sped towards the woman. The car quickly veered off in the opposite direction. It was dark and there were no street lights out here, so Jeff hadn't gotten a good look at the car or the driver. All he could tell was that the car was a dark-colored sedan.

Anger flared inside Jeff's chest and he shouted as the car tore off. He pounded the steering wheel in indignation, wanting nothing more than to chase the attacker down and force him to answer for his crimes. But it had been too dark to get a license plate, and this girl needed his help right now.

He slammed on the brakes, pulled his car across the road between the girl and potential oncoming cars, and jumped out, glancing again at his cell phone. No service. Of course, they were in the middle of nowhere.

Shoving the phone back in his pocket, he took another look at the girl, surprised when he saw she was more woman than girl. He checked her vital signs, relieved when he found a steady but very weak pulse. She was still breathing, barely. Her face, which would otherwise be pretty, had some old and fresh bruising and some small cuts. She was abnormally thin and pale. Her clothing was worn and too big, and she wasn't wearing shoes. Angry red lines from a rope or some other restraint wrapped around her wrists. She didn't seem to have any broken bones, but she was banged up pretty badly.

What had happened to this girl? Who had done this to her?

Rage coursed through Jeff's veins, and his protective instincts kicked into overdrive. He would find that guy, or whoever did this to her and make them pay. He wanted to hunt them down and do to them whatever they did to her, but he wouldn't be allowed to do that. Until they were arrested, all he could do for her now was protect her.

He gently scooped up the girl in his arms and brought her to his truck, laying her on the back seat and awkwardly buckling her in. Jeff slammed the truck door and flew down the street at record speed.

Luckily Estella had brought her own car to the campsite, so Jeff would call her once he got cell phone reception. First, he needed to call the local police. He held his phone again and groaned. Still no service.

Out in the woods near the campsite, a hospital wasn't exactly close by. Jeff didn't know how long he had been driving, but it seemed like hours later when he rolled into the hospital parking lot. He pulled in to the emergency room entrance and carried the girl inside.

"Help! She was hit by a car," Jeff called out. A few nurses rushed towards him with a gurney, and he laid her down on it gently, instinctively smoothing her dark hair back from her face before they wheeled her down the hall. Jeff began to follow, but a tired-looking nurse held up her hand to stop him. Jeff stumbled to a stop so he wouldn't slam into her.

"You can't come in while we treat her, sir. Are you family?" She adjusted her rectangle glasses.

"No. I found her at the scene."

"Okay. You can wait out here or leave your contact information at the front desk. Then we can let you know how she is doing later on." With that, she shuffled down the hall where the other nurses had taken the girl.

Jeff let out a deep breath. There wasn't much he could do at this point except park his car and wait. He would wait for the girl until he could speak to her.

Now that he finally had cell phone reception, he called the local police station to report the crime, which had been attempted murder and a possible kidnapping case.

Well, his vacation would have to wait. He'd been working at the Covert Police Detectives Unit in Portland, Maine, until he reenlisted in the Marines. After over a year of searching for terrorists in the desert, he'd been looking forward to time off at the Kennebunk beach house he and his sister had inherited. He needed to recover from a year's worth of dust, bullets, scorching sun, and the haunting memories that kept him awake at night. This time off was supposed to be for mourning the recent death of his father before he'd return to work at the Covert Police Detectives Unit, but Jeff knew his father would have wanted him to take care of this girl to be priority. He would wait all night here if he had to until he found out how the girl was doing.

He dialed Estella's number and she picked up. "Estella, I'm not coming back to the campsite. I'm at the hospital."

"What? What happened?" Estella cried. "Are you okay?"

It looked like they weren't going to be having coffee and s'mores after all.

CHAPTER TWO

The woman tried to open her eyes and found out that they felt like lead weights had been placed on top of them. When she finally got them open she was in a strange room with a very unpleasant smell. A strange staccato noise repeated rhythmically. A dull pain throbbed in her head, ribs, and legs. Every part of her body hurt, and it felt like she was being weighed down.

She wondered where she was and how she got here, looking at her hand and frowning as she saw the line that snaked from the I.V bag hanging over her bed. In the distance, she heard voices and tried to lift her head to see who it was. She couldn't and in the end, she gave up and rested her head on the pillow. She heard the sound of her door being opened and sighed in relief. She was finally going to get some answers and she needed a lot of those.

"Hey, how are you feeling?" a warm voice asked.

The woman looked up to see two other women standing beside her bed. She knew they were nurses from the clothes they wore. Which meant she was in the hospital. Of course, she was, something she should have figured out already from the smell and tubes sticking out of her arms.

"You've been through a lot, haven't you?" the other nurse said as she checked the IV bag.

The woman said nothing, still too disoriented to make sense of what they were saying. Her head hurt and her whole body felt stiff.

"Don't worry," one of the nurses attending to her said, "it's okay if you don't feel like talking yet. Rest and take it easy, okay?"

"Where am I and how did I get here?" the woman asked.

The two nurses exchanged a look before they turned to face the woman.

"Actually, we were hoping you'll help us with that. What do you remember about the incident?"

The woman frowned. "What incident?"

Again the nurses exchanged the same look before they turned around and looked at the woman again.

"What's your name?"

"My name...? My name is..." the woman paused, her mouth hanging open for a few seconds. No name formed in her mouth or brain. "I... I don't know," she whispered.

If you enjoyed this sample, check out the book here on Amazon or just search for Ashley Emma on Amazon:
https://www.amazon.com/gp/product/B07SDSFV3J
Thanks for reading!

Made in the USA
Las Vegas, NV
26 May 2022

49386934R00178